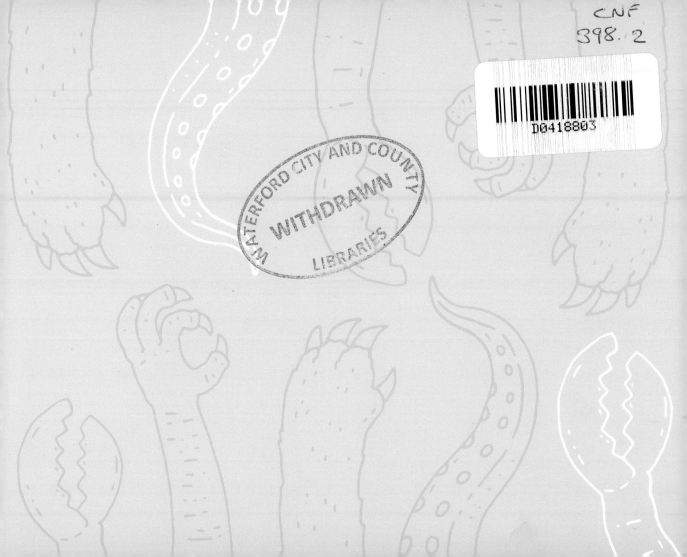

First published in the
United Kingdom in 2016 by
Portico
1 Gower Street
London
WC1E 6HD

An imprint of Pavilion Books Company Ltd

ISBN 978-1-91023-284-2

A CIP catalogue record for this book is available
from the British Library.

10 9 8 7 6 5 4 3 2 1

Reproduction by Mission Productions Ltd, Hong Kong
Printed and bound by Times Offset (Malaysia) Sdn Bhd

This book can be ordered direct from the
publisher at www.pavilionbooks.com

CooL MyTHoLogy

MALCOLM CROFT

FiLLed with FaNTasTIc facts FoR kiDs oF aLL Ages

Contents

Welcome to the world of
COOL MYTHOLOGY!

In order for you to understand all the amazing mythologies of the world, and learn about what mythology actually is, you'll have to travel back in time to the very beginning of human history. But that won't be enough. You'll have to travel forward into the future to catch a glimpse of the destruction of the world. But even that won't be enough. You'll also have to travel to other dimensions, other realms, and deep within your own imagination.

Myths come in all shapes and sizes. From folklore and legends, monsters to beasts, allegories to metaphors, myths and mythological ideas permeate every part of the world, every language and every culture, no matter how different they are. They help us understand our past, and they help us identify with our humanity, no matter what

part of the world we happen to live in. From Native American folklores to Arthurian legends, from stories told by African tribes to ancient Greek tales, myths help us understand our place in the world – and the many other realms that could be more than just fantasy. All myths are rooted in the basic human desire to understand the world around us, and to understand a culture's unique mythology is to understand your world just a little better.

Ahead of you is a long but heroic quest. It is a journey of self-discovery, and one in which, come the end, you'll have reached a better understanding of the world.

So before we begin, take a deep breath and rub your eyes … things are about to get a little bit weird. But that's a good thing. Enjoy!

'Heaven and Hell are within us,
and all the gods are within us...
They are magnified dreams,
and dreams are manifestations
in image form of the energies of the
body in conflict with each other.
That is what myth is.'

Joseph Campbell, *The Power of Myth*

Map of World Mythology

Let's go on a journey through time and space, travelling around the entire world, and see how many mythologies we can find ...

NORTH AMERICA

There are many North American myths that have wandered around the landscape. From the Ho-Chuck, Cherokee, Choctaw, Iroquois, Seneca and Creek tribes of the east Atlantic, through to the Blackfoot, Pawnee, Lakota and Crow stories of the centre of America, and finally, the Kwakiutl, Nootka, Lummi and Haida tribes of Pacific west America.

MESOAMERICAN

There are other cool Mesoamerican myths to check out too. The Teotihuacan, Monte-Alto, Olmec, Mayan and Aztec myths all have similar deities to the Incan mythologies, that existed in countries such as El Salvador, Honduras, Costa Rica, Mexico, Belize and Nicaragua.

SOUTH AMERICA

The Incas were not the only South American civilisation with a rich mythology. In the nearby Amazon Rainforest, the Achagua, Guarani, Wayuu, Pemon and Carib cultures all had a rich mythology relating to their creation.

MEDITERRANEAN

The Romans and Greeks may have the most famous characters, but there is a whole collection of gods and deities from this region.

MIDDLE EAST

Following the reign of Zoroastrianism, Persia changed its belief to Islam, but other mythologies including Kurdish, Ossetian and Armenian also sprang to life.

INDIA

Originating in Northern India, near the mighty river Indus (from where Hinduism takes its name), Hindu mythology has been called the world's oldest belief system.

NORTH AFRICA

North African mythology encompasses Ancient Egypt, the Nubian mythology of Sudan and the ancient Berber culture, which still exists today in countries such as Morocco.

9

Something out of Nothing

From intelligent design to multiverse theories, from Genesis to Brahma, from Scandinavian fire demons to the Aboriginal Rainbow Serpent, or whatever else you can think of, there are many ideas on how life, the Universe and everything popped into creation.

Creation myths are the most common forms of myths in the world's cultures. They date back to the earliest times when these cultures first evolved, and thoughts immediately turned to 'Where are we?' and 'How did we get here?' and, most importantly, 'Where are we going?'

A God Named Pangu

Many cultures around the world, from Egypt to China, Finland to Polynesia, believe in the cosmic egg creation myth. In China, for example, the myth of Pangu, developed by Taoist monks more than 3,000 years ago, says the Universe began as an egg. A god named Pangu, born inside the egg, broke the shell into two halves: the upper half became the sky, while the lower half became the Earth. As the god grew in size, the sky and the Earth grew too and were separated further. When Pangu died, his body became different parts of the Earth.

King Indian: Brahma

Brahma is the god of creation in Hinduism, a religion practised mainly in India. Brahma has four faces, north, east, south and west, and was brought into being by thought alone, first creating knowledge and then the Universe. He was born in a golden egg and its two halves became Heaven and Earth. When Brahma became lonely he divided himself into two forms, male and female. This division will continue until all life has been created, then the god Shiva will destroy the world, and Brahma will create a new one – and the cycle will continue.

BANG!!

The Five Types

In mythology, there are, in general, five classifications of creation myths:

Creation Ex Nihilo (Something out of Nothing)

A Divine Being, such as God, created the whole Universe out of nothing.

Emergence

An origin story that tells how life on Earth has passed through a series of worlds and transformed over time until reaching where we are now.

World Parent

Where two parents, the sky (male) and earth (female), for example, or light and dark, merge together to breathe life into the Earth.

Earth Diver

A creature, usually a bird or reptile, is sent to Earth by a 'creator' and life as we know it grows from the aftermath of that animal plunging to Earth. Common in Native American folklore.

Cosmogony

The Universe, and everything in it, was created by the splitting of 'Heaven' and 'Earth' into two separate places, or the cracking of a cosmic egg, or a bringing of order from chaos.

Mother Nature

Gaia – the Greek primordial goddess or the first female deity, also known as Earth Mother, Mother Nature, Mother of the Titans, and one of the Immortals – is the starting point of Greek mythology.

In the Beginning

The ancient Greek people had a strong desire to create stories and work out where they originated from. They devised creation myths, such as Gaia, that resonate to this day.

Born out of Chaos, Gaia was the first deity of Greek mythology, out of whom all other gods were born.

It is the union of Gaia and Uranus that produced the Titans (see page 24) and the children of the Titans became known as the Olympians (see page 42).

Greek Mythology Family Tree

According to Greek mythology, the ancient Greek gods and goddesses consisted of three major dynasties from different generations:

The first generation of ancient Greek gods were the primeval deities, the Immortals, of which Gaia is one. These gods existed at the beginning of time and lived within a place in the Universe known as the Elemental Chaos.

The second generation of ancient Greek gods were the Titans.

The third generation of ancient Greek gods were the Olympians.

Mythnomer

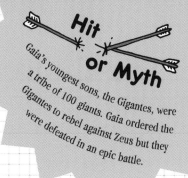

Hit or Myth

Gaia's youngest sons, the Gigantes, were a tribe of 100 giants. Gaia ordered the Gigantes to rebel against Zeus but they were defeated in an epic battle.

The Immortals, the primeval gods of Greek mythology, were a race of giants. These 'elder gods' were known as:

☆ **Gaia**
Mother Nature
☆ **Erebus**
God of darkness and the Underworld
☆ **Tartarus**
God of the abyss beneath the Underworld
☆ **Eros**
God of procreation
☆ **Pontus**
God of the sea
☆ **Uranus**
God of the sky and the heavens

The Theory of Nothing

Cosmogony is any model concerning the origin of either the cosmos, or the so-called reality of sentient beings.

In Greece, by Mount Parnassus, lie the ancient ruins of Delphi. Known as the supreme oracle site of the ancient Mediterranean world, it is believed to be a place sacred to Gaia, and was guarded by her serpent daughter, Python (yes, from which snakes take their name!), as well as the 'centre of the Earth' according to the Titan god Zeus (one of Gaia's 12 children).

The Children of the Sun

The Sun plays an extremely large part in many of the world's most enduring mythologies. In Egyptian and Incan mythology, for example, it was not a bright yellow star dangling in the sky more than 90 million miles away, but a god from which all life springs forth ...

Mesoamerican Myths

The Children of the Sun was the first Mesoamerican culture's creation myth, a story that was passed down orally through many generations to describe the start of the famous Incan Empire that existed more than 800 years ago. The Incan people could not understand how the Sun, stars and life – plant, animal and human – all began, so a man called Manco Capac, an early civilised Incan ruler (and possibly mythical himself!), started the Children of the Sun myth as a way of explaining where the Incan people came from ... and how they could better themselves.

The Inca believed the mountains in the Andes had a god who lived within them.

Inti: Ancient Incan Sun God

Inti, the ancient Incan Sun god, was a hugely important part of the Incan Empire, a civilisation of people that originated in the 13th and 14th centuries in the countries now known as Peru, Ecuador, Bolivia, Chile, Argentina and Columbia. To the Incas, Inti was the primary source of all that was good in the world.

The most important gods in Incan mythology were:

1. **Inti**
   Sun god

2. **Viracocha**
   Creator god

3. **Illapa**
   Weather/thunder god

4. **Pachamama**
   Earth goddess

5. **Mamacocha**
   Sea goddess

6. **Mamaquilla**
   Moon goddess, Inti's wife

The Rise of the Sun Myth

The Children of the Sun myth tells of a time when people lived on the Earth without any rules or clothes, and people weren't very nice to each other.

The myth goes that the Sun god, Inti, saw what was happening on Earth, and taught his two children – Manco Capac (son) and Mama Ocllo (daughter) – in the art of civilisation and sent them to Earth to teach people how to live properly and to build a capital city, a place to worship Inti. And from this the revered Incan civilisation began. The Incan people were taught many skills by Manco and Mama who, in turn, became worshipped as living gods, and their family dynasty ruled the Incan Empire for more than 300 years. Incan civilisation started from this Sun myth and shows how myths can transform societies.

MYTH BUSTER

The Incan Empire is revered as one of the most intelligent civilisations in history – they were the first to farm potatoes, perform complex surgery, build earthquake-defying houses, and they created a road system more than 18,000 miles (28,967km) long.

The Rainbow Serpent

From cosmic eggs cracking in two, to the worshipping of the Children of the Sun, there are many creation myths that seem weird at first, but then make sense the more you learn about them. Snake worship, and the Rainbow Serpent, is the perfect example of this.

Dreamtime Dreaming

According to Aboriginal mythologies throughout Australia, all human, animal and fish life is part of the same divine being, a being that connects the human, physical and sacred worlds. The Dreamtime mythology is their understanding of this world and how it came to be. The Dreamtime is perceived as the beginning of knowledge, much like the Children of the Sun in Incan Civilisation. From understanding the Dreamtime, believers can come to learn the laws of existence, and knowledge of these laws can help them survive.

The Dreamtime began when Ancestor Beings, such as the Rainbow Serpent or Kangaroo, emerged from within the Earth at the beginning of everything, the creation point. These supernatural beings were born into a world that had a flat surface and was in total darkness. These beings travelled across the barren world creating landscapes, such as mountains, rivers, trees and lakes. They made people, animals and the natural elements of water, air and fire. They made the Sun, the Moon and the stars. At the end of all this creation, the Ancestor Beings sank back into the Earth to sleep.

The Dreamtime creation story lives on in the spiritual lives of Aboriginal people's traditions, and the creation of the Earth is performed in regular ceremonies, songs and dances, accompanied by a didgeridoo!

Hit or Myth

To the Gagudju people in the tropical north of Australia, the Rainbow Serpent was called Almudj and was their creator being. Today, Almudj is still viewed as a great creator, responsible for bringing the wet season each year, which causes all forms of life to flourish and appears in the sky as a rainbow. Almudj, however, is also to be feared as he can punish anyone who has been bad, by drowning them in floods.

The Rainbow Serpent is the anthropomorphism of a river in a dry, desert environment, as it snakes and meanders its way bringing water – with its life-sustaining properties – to the land. In some cultures in Australia the Rainbow Serpent is considered to be the ultimate creator of everything in the Universe.

The Roots of Africa

Africa is the second largest continent in the world. Home to 54 countries, hundreds of diverse cultures and more than 1,000 different languages spoken by more than a billion people, Africa is quite simply huge. Although no single mythology dominates, or unites, this historically rich landscape, different ethnic groups and peoples share some common beliefs.

Rich History

Africa's greatest mythologies are famous for their many different narratives that deal with the afterlife and the origin of the Universe, but they are revered by their fascinating attachment to magic, spirit animals and celestial beings, as well as loads of terrifying local legends and witchcraft!

The Legend of God

Africa is stuffed to the sand dunes with hundreds of gods, all of whom go by different names in different countries and regions. Opposite is a list of some of them to get you started. Look at a map of Africa, and find out who believes in which god and where.

Adu Ogyinae

According to the mythology of the Akan tribe – with around 20 million people, who now reside in East Guinea – all humans used to live deep underneath the Earth's surface. One day, seven men, five women, a leopard and a dog crawled out of a hole made by a massive worm, and looked upon the world for the first time. The first man to climb out – Adu Ogyinae – seemed to immediately understand the world around him, almost as if by magic, whereas the others were terrified of all they saw.

Adu gave the group strength by laying his hands on them. He became known as the leader of the first group of humans – a belief that is still deeply held today.

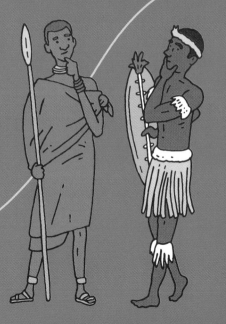

Deity	People and region	Role
Ala	Ibo, Nigeria	Mother goddess, ruler of the Underworld, goddess of fertility
Amma	Dogon, Mali	Supreme god
Cagn	Bushmen, Southwest Africa	Creator god
Eshu	Yoruba, Nigeria	Trickster and messenger god
Katonda	Buganda, East Africa	Creator god, father of the gods, king and judge of the Universe
Kibuka	Buganda, East Africa	War god
Leza	Bantu, Central and South Africa	Creator and sky god
Mujaji	Lovedu, South Africa	Rain goddess
Nyame	Ashanti and Akan, Ghana	Creator god associated with the Sun and Moon
Olorun	Yoruba, West Africa	All-knowing deity

The Science of Mythology

Myths and legends are a vital part of human existence; of what it means to be human. They tell us of a time when gods co-habited with humans, heavenly voices could be heard and visions of the future could be seen. But, because they're just stories, they can be deconstructed, pulled apart and analysed, in the hope that we can understand them better, and to separate the fact from the fiction …

Deconstructing a Myth

If you've ever tried to write your own myth – and you should, it's fun! – you would quickly realise that your story will fit into one of the seven basic plots of storytelling.

So let's take a look at these seven narratives. Then think of your ten favourite books, or films, or stories, and work out which of the seven narratives they belong to.

From *Beowulf*, the most epic of all epic hero quests.

MYTHQUOTED

'His father's warrior were wound round his heart/With golden rings, bound to their prince/By his father's treasure. So young men build/The future, wisely open-handed in peace, /Protected in war; so warriors earn/Their fame, and wealth is shaped with a sword.'

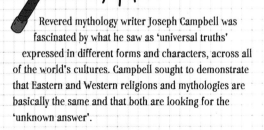

Revered mythology writer Joseph Campbell was fascinated by what he saw as 'universal truths' expressed in different forms and characters, across all of the world's cultures. Campbell sought to demonstrate that Eastern and Western religions and mythologies are basically the same and that both are looking for the 'unknown answer'.

The seven basic plots in myths

#1 Defeating a Monster
A hero, or protagonist, sets out to defeat an evil force or being or creature, which usually threatens the hero's homeland or family.

#2 Rags to Riches/Riches to Rags
The hero aims to collect as much power, wealth or love interest as possible, only to lose it all, but becomes a better person in the process. For Riches to Rags, the process is reversed, but the conclusion is the same.

#3 The Quest
The hero (often with companions) sets out to locate an object of great importance, or to find a special location. Along the way, they face many obstacles and temptations.

#4 Voyage and Return
The hero goes to a strange land and, after overcoming all the threats it poses, returns with nothing but experience.

#5 Comedy
A character with a sense of humour overcomes adversity and the story concludes with a happy or cheerful ending.

#6 Tragedy
The protagonist is an evil person who falls from grace and whose death is welcomed by everyone (often including the protagonist).

#7 Rebirth
An important event forces the story's protagonist to change their ways, often making them a better person.

The Romans Are Coming!

For centuries, the ancient Greeks, and their way of thinking, ruled the world. Then the Romans came along, took over the world and also appropriated Greek mythology (not to mention ancient Egyptian mythology) as their own.

Greek vs Roman

Fascinated by the myths the Greeks had woven around their gods and goddesses, the Romans gradually changed some of their gods, or *numina* as they called them:

Romulus vs Remus

The Founding of Rome, unarguably one of the most evocative stories about the founding of one the most important cities on the planet, is actually a myth. But it's a good one. The story belongs to two mythical characters, Romulus and Remus, twin brothers born to the Roman god of war, Mars. Abandoned as infants, the twins were raised by a she-wolf. After reclaiming a throne for their maternal grandfather, the boys decided to establish their own city. It wasn't long before they got into a massive fight about where the city would be located. During the dispute, Romulus killed Remus. He would later lay the foundations for Rome – the capital city of the Roman Empire – and the myth of his creation of Rome would come to encapsulate the ideals, and moral values, of the city. Many modern historians now believe the city came first, and the myth followed after.

Greek	Roman	Description
Zeus	Jupiter	Supreme ruler of the gods. Threw lightning bolts!
Poseidon	Neptune	God of the sea, brother of Zeus. Wielded a three-pronged spear known as a trident.
Hades	Pluto	God of the Underworld and the dead, brother of Zeus. Wore a helmet which rendered its wearer invisible.
Ares	Mars	God of War and son of Zeus and Hera.
Athena	Minerva	Daughter of Zeus. The protector of civilised life, handicrafts and agriculture.
Apollo	Apollo	Son of Zeus. Master musician, archer god, healer, god of light, god of truth, Sun god.
Aphrodite	Venus	Daughter of Uranus. Goddess of love and beauty.
Hermes	Mercury	Son of Zeus. Wore wings on his sandals and his hat.
Artemis	Diana	Apollo's twin sister and daughter of Zeus. As Apollo is the Sun, so Artemis is the Moon.
Hephaestus	Vulcan	Son of Hera, god of fire. The only ugly and deformed god.

Hit or Myth

In Roman mythology, Pluto was the god of the Underworld and death. He was the brother of Juno, Jupiter, Vesta, Neptune and Ceres. The gods of the Underworld were called the *di inferi*, meaning the infernal gods. His Greek counterpart was called Hades.

The Mighty Titans

The Titans were the first generation of gods and goddesses who ruled supreme over the Universe, according to ancient Greek mythology. These Titanides were the descendants of the first primordial gods, Gaia and Uranus, who were in turn born out of Chaos.

The 12 Titans

The ancient Greeks had a strong fascination with creation, and to fulfil their need to know where they came from, they developed a myth which explained where the main gods and goddesses of their religion originated and what their relationships were to each other. The Greek creation myth started with Chaos, then the primeval gods who produced the Titans, from whom the 12 Olympian gods descended. The first generation of 12 Titans are:

The Second Generation

The second generation of Titans consisted of the children of the first 12 Titans: Hyperion's children Helios, Selene and Eos; Coeus' children Lelantos, Leto and Asteria; Iapetus' sons Atlas, Prometheus, Epimetheus and Menoetius; Oceanus' daughter Metis; and Crius' sons Astraeus, Pallas and Perses.

★ **Cronus** Leader of the first generation of Titans.

★ **Rhea** The goddess of fertility and the mother of gods.

★ **Coeus** The god of intelligence.

★ **Phoebe** The goddess of the Moon.

★ **Hyperion** The lord of light.

★ **Theia** The mother of the Sun and goddess of all that glitters (gold, silver and gems).

★ **Iapetus** The god of mortal life (his consort was Clymene).

★ **Oceanus** The lord of the ocean.

★ **Tethys** The goddess of the rivers.

★ **Mnemosyne** The goddess of memory and the inventor of words.

★ **Crius** The god of the constellations.

★ **Themis** The goddess of justice and order.

Mythnomer

The word 'titanic' originates from the great size and power of the Titans, while the word 'ocean' derives from the Titan god Oceanus, lord of the sea.

The 12 Titans are believed to represent the important natural and spiritual aspects of life. This first generation of Titans were a race of powerful giants who eventually lost control over the Universe to their children, the Olympians (see page 42).

The Titanomachy

When it comes to epic battles, forget *Star Wars*, *Harry Potter* and *Spider-Man*. Whether it's a fight between gods and monsters, demons and demon-hunters, wizards and witches, or giants and very tiny people, all the world mythologies love a cosmic fight between good and evil. But the winner that beats them all is …

Hit or Myth

Atlas, one of the Titans, was condemned by Zeus to bear the weight of the world on his shoulders. This is why the word 'Atlas' was used to describe a book of maps.

Wrath of the Titans

In the blue corner, the Titans. In the red corner, the Olympians. It's the most famous battle between Greek gods and goddesses and one that would never be rivalled.

The stage for this mega-fight was set when the youngest Titan, Cronus, overthrew his own father, Uranus (ruler of the cosmos), with the help of his mother, Gaia (Mother Nature, see page 12).

The Titanomachy (or war of the Titans) was a ten-year-long series of mythological wars, and whoever won would rule the Universe! According to the Greek poem *Theogony*, the battles were brutal, with many Titans eventually being cast down to Tartarus, a deep abyss used as a dungeon for the wicked (our concept of Hell) for all eternity. Emerging victorious, the Olympian gods (and brothers) Zeus, Poseidon and Hades divided the world among themselves and ruled the Universe.

The war didn't end there, though. After the Titanomachy, Gaia freed her children the Gigantes, a race of giants, from imprisonment in order to restore the rule of the defeated Titans, and a battle between the Olympians and the Gigantes began. This was the Gigantomachy.

MYTH BUSTER

There are many super-battles in mythology. Check these out too!

⭐ **The Mahabharata** Hindu
⭐ **Armageddon** Christian
⭐ **Battle of Banquan** First battle in Chinese history
⭐ **Battle of Mag Itha** Celtic
⭐ **Battle of Zhoulu** Second battle in Chinese history
⭐ **Battle of Bravellir** Swedes vs Danes!
⭐ **Cath Magd Tuired** Celtic
⭐ **Trojan War** Greeks vs Trojans!

Hit or Myth

Who would win in a fight between Odin and Zeus? Or Quetzacoatl and Brahma? Or the Great Spirit and Ahuda Mazda? The word used to describe battles between gods is 'Theomachy'.

Here Be Monsters #1

As fascinating as gods are in mythology, the real reason why many mythologies of the world have endured is because of its monsters. These days you can't move for a legendary monster movie, or an origin story of mythology's greatest evil creatures. What is it about mythical monsters – the stuff of nightmares! – that is just so cool?

Lycanthropes

Lycanthropes, or werewolves or man-wolves – 'wer' is an Old English term for 'man' – are among the oldest creatures in mythology. Famous legends from all around the world tell tales of men who turn into wolves on nights where the Moon is full, and then back into human form again. In their animal form, werewolves were bloodthirsty creatures that devoured people, ripping them to shreds. Stories of werewolves reflect our universal emotions about the more 'animal' aspects of human nature and our behaviour. Transformation legends, such as werewolves and berserkers, perhaps originated when our nomadic ancestors wore animal skins and masks and performed rituals. The Greek writer Ovid told a myth of how a Greek king called Lycaon was transformed into a wolf as punishment for serving human flesh to the gods.

The Lightning Bird

The Impundulu, or Lightning Bird as it is known in South African mythology, is a supernatural bird from Pondo, Zulu and Xhosa folklore. As big as a human, the Impundulu can summon lightning and storms. As a shape-shifter the bird can appear as a human. But watch out – the Impundulu attacks people and likes the taste of human blood.

Hit or Myth

If you had to invent a mythological monster, what would you call it? And what sort would it be?

Mythnomer

The word 'monster' comes from the Latin *monstrum*, meaning 'a sign of future events'.

Ninki Nanka

The Ninki Nanka is a monster that, so the legend goes, lives in the swamps of the Gambia River in East Africa. It is a dragon-like creature with the body of a crocodile, the head of a horse (but with horns!) and a long neck like a giraffe. Oh, and it's not small either, at up to 50ft (15.2m) long!

The Gods of Egypt #1

Western mythology was born in Egypt. Nearly 2,000 years before the ancient Greeks began deciding the names of their Immortals, the pharaohs and kings of ancient Egypt had already developed a mythology system with more than 2,000 deities, many of whose names you will recognise ...

Amun

Horus

Osiris

Back to the Future

Egyptian gods and goddesses were worshipped for more than 3,000 years. Ancient Egyptian civilisation, a period that saw stunning advances in human development in agriculture, construction and medicine, began when the Nile Valley region of Egypt became ruled by a leader who unified Egypt. The pharaohs (rulers) of Egypt were worshipped as living gods, with ancient Egyptians believing they were the sons, or prophets, of the divine.

How ancient Egyptian creation mythology was invented – in ten easy steps!

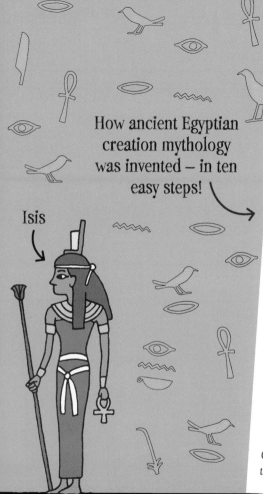

Isis

⭐ **1** In the beginning, there were only the dark waters of chaos, known as Nun.

⭐ **2** One day, a hill known as Ben-Ben rose up out of these waters.

⭐ **3** Standing atop this hill was Atum, the first god, the god of Sun and creation.

⭐ **4** Atum coughed, and out of his mouth came Shu, the god of the air, and Tefnut, the goddess of moisture.

⭐ **5** Shu and Tefnut had two children: Geb, the god of the Earth, and Nut, the goddess of the sky. Shu lifted Nut up, so that she became a protective canopy over Geb.

⭐ **6** Nut and Geb had four children: Osiris, Isis, Seth and Nephthys.

⭐ **7** Osiris became king of the Earth, Isis the queen. Osiris ruled over the Earth for thousands of years. He was a good king.

⭐ **8** Seth became jealous and angry at Osiris. He wanted to be the ruler of the Earth! He killed Osiris. Osiris was sent to the Underworld. Seth became king.

⭐ **9** Osiris and his queen Isis had a son called Horus. Horus fought Seth in an epic battle and regained the throne.

⭐ **10** Horus became the king of the Earth, and Osiris, his father, remains king of the Underworld to this day.

Hit or Myth

Ancient Egyptians preserved the bodies of the dead so that the soul could reunite with its body and properly enjoy the afterlife. When preparing a body for mummification, the embalmer would pull the brain out through the nose using a long metal hook.

A Siren's Call

The world is made up of 75 per cent water. The world's oceans account for more than 90 per cent of that water. Scientists believe that we have only searched 5 per cent of the world's oceans so far. It's not entirely unreasonable to believe, then, that somewhere in the world's waterways are sirens, mermaids, harpies and undines lurking in the dark deep, waiting for their next human to entice ...

In German folklore, there was a story of a golden-haired beauty named Lorelei who threw herself into the deadly River Rhine, after an unhappy love affair. Following her death, a ghostly Lorelei could be seen sitting on a rock in the river, singing sweet lullabies to passing ships. Sailors, transfixed by her dulcet tones, begin sailing towards her, only to hit the rocks and sink to their doom.

Mermaids, Mermen and Manatees

The famous physical appearance of mermaids and mermen, with the torso of a human and the tail of a fish, has captivated sailors, fishermen and water-dwellers for centuries, and their supposed existence has infiltrated almost every mythology on the planet. Most legends and folklores, no matter where you go, will have a story of a bewitching siren or water-maiden wanting you to come play in the water with her. From the Lady of the Lake of Arthurian legend, to the morgans of France (who can rise to the surface of the sea to cuddle fishermen only to sometimes take them down and force them to live in their watery homes with them – or worse, kill them), there are many mermaid myths out there. The first written account of a half-fish, half-human hybrid is Oannes, a Babylonian god from the 4th century BC, who would leave the sea every day and return at night.

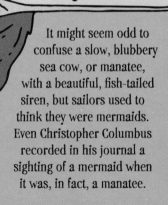

Mythnomer

It might seem odd to confuse a slow, blubbery sea cow, or manatee, with a beautiful, fish-tailed siren, but sailors used to think they were mermaids. Even Christopher Columbus recorded in his journal a sighting of a mermaid when it was, in fact, a manatee.

Jason and the Argonauts

Living on an island surrounded by rocks, Sirens were sea nymphs who sang so beautifully that passing sailors became enchanted by their songs and would steer their ships towards them, wrecking their boats on the rocks. In their quest to find the Golden Fleece, Jason and the Argonauts sailed close to the Sirens' island. When they heard the nymphs' beautiful voices, one of the crew, Orpheus, played his lyre to drown out the sound.

My Kingdom for a Horse!

Achilles, Paris, Hector, Ajax. They're all here. The Greek Trojan War is the coolest mythological story in popular culture, with all the most recognisable names of Greek mythology. Most prominently told through Homer's *Iliad* and the *Odyssey* (written around 700BC), the Trojan War teaches us – through metaphor, allegory and symbolism – many of the virtues, and pitfalls, of what it means to be human. It's also a great story of war, strategy and revenge …

War? What Is It Good For?

The Trojan War was waged after a Trojan prince (Paris) stole the wife (Helen, also the daughter of Zeus) from Menelaus, King of Sparta, a powerful Greek city. The war was a ten-year-long conflict that saw Greek warriors lay siege to Troy. Homer's epic poem, the *Iliad*, describes the strategies and cunning activities the gods, goddesses and human heroes carried out during the final year of the war. Rooted in Paris' vanity and passion for Helen, the war teaches us how those two ideas can lead us to temptation, and ultimately to our downfall.

The Trojan War

After ten long years, the Greeks had still not rescued Helen. The tall and strong city walls that protected Troy were impregnable.

Not ones to give up, the Greeks built a large wooden horse beyond the city walls. When the horse was complete, the Greek army sailed away, leaving the horse behind. The people of Troy wanted to burn the horse, but Priam (the king) ordered the horse to be brought inside the city walls as a symbol of their victory! As the Trojans slept, the Greeks inside the horse crept out and opened the city gates for the rest of the army who had secretly returned. They recaptured Helen and returned her to Sparta.

MYTH BUSTER

The ancient Greeks thought that the Trojan War was a real historical event that had taken place in the 13th or 12th century BC. Many modern scholars think that the story of the Trojan War may have had a real basis, and became a myth with the passing of time.

MYTHQUOTED

'Was this the face that launch'd a thousand ships/And burnt the topless towers of Ilium? /Sweet Helen, make me immortal with a kiss.'

From Christopher Marlowe's Doctor Faustus

The Wooden Horse Fact File

★ It would have been around 10ft (3m) wide, based on the width of the widest gate discovered in the ruins of Troy.

★ The total weight might have been around 2 tons empty. With just 20 fully armed warriors inside, weighing around 15st (95.2kg) each, this would have at least doubled the weight.

★ Most ancient Greeks believed there were 30–40 warriors hidden inside the horse!

★ The wooden horse bore an inscription: *'For their return home, the Greeks dedicate this offering to Athena'.*

Here Be Monsters #2

The Meaning of Monsters

Monsters have roared and ravaged, clawed and crushed, torn and thundered their way into the world's myths and legends. Defeating a monster is one of the most common narratives in the whole canon of mythological stories. A hero's quest to overcome an evil creature still ranks as one of the most popular stories ever told. Monsters have come to represent everything that's scary about the natural world and the darkest corners of human imagination. They embody evil, in all the forms and shapes it can transform into. We have personified our natural fears into the minds of these mythological monsters, and they challenge us, as the heroes and heroines of our own myths, to go on our own quests for survival.

MYTHQUOTED

'At the source of the Amimone grows a plane tree, beneath which, they say, the Hydra (water snake) grew. I am ready to believe that this beast was superior in size to other water snakes, and that its poison had something in it so deadly that Heracles (Hercules) treated the points of his arrows with its gall.'

Pausanias, c. 150AD

The Hydra

In Greek mythology, the Hydra was a giant water snake with nine heads. Doesn't sound too bad? Well, one of the heads was immortal! The Hydra lived in the murky waters of Lerna in the land of Argos. Defeating the Hydra was the second of Hercules' famous 12 labours. However, when one of the Hydra's heads was cut off, two more grew in its place. Tricky! To overcome the monster, Hercules called on his friend Iolaus for assistance. As soon as Hercules cut off a head, Iolaus would cauterise the wound with a hot iron so no heads could grow back. After removing the Hydra's immortal head, Hercules buried it under a large rock, where it remains to this day …

Kraken

The Kraken is a giant sea monster said to dwell off the coast of Norway. A huge part of Norse mythology, the Kraken was up to 1½ miles (2.4km) long and said to look either like a crab or a squid. While it had no magical powers, the Kraken's sheer size created huge whirlpools when it went back under the waves that were enough to suck in boats from hundreds of miles away.

Weapons of Choice

Sword, shields, hammers, spears, bows, blades, axes, clubs, rings, potions and stones – in all of the world's most magical mythologies there are lots of terrifying ways to stun, defend against, attack and cause harm to your mythical enemy.

HAMMER TIME

In Norse mythology, Thor is the god of thunder and protector of the Earth who wields a magical hammer, called Mjolnir, meaning 'crusher'. Mjolnir is the most fearsome weapon in Norse lore, capable of destroying mountains with one smash. It's said to have been made by blacksmith dwarf brothers Sindri and Brokkr.

THE MOST FAMOUS SWORD IN THE WORLD

Excalibur is the sword that the legendary, heroic King Arthur wielded in his famous battles alongside his Knights of the Round Table, against all invaders of Britain, somewhere around the 5th and 6th century AD. As a boy, Arthur came across a magical sword in a stone; extracting the sword helped him make a claim as the rightful King of England. Excalibur has many special powers like cutting through steel and rock.

ACHILLES' SHIELD

This is the shield that Achilles, a powerful warrior of Greek mythology, uses in his fight with Hector, the Prince of Troy, famously described in a passage in the epic poem the *Iliad* by Homer, depicting the legend of the Trojan War.

Homer gives a detailed description of the shield's decorative layers, a series of contrasts – war and peace, work and play, kings and farmers – which many myth-torians believe is a metaphor for keeping the entire world safe and protected. For Achilles, the strongest and bravest hero warrior that ever lived, it is the perfect weapon to keep the peace. A pity it couldn't protect his heel!

THE TRIDENT

The trident is a weapon that keeps cropping up in myth and legend. In many classic depictions of the Devil, he is seen carrying the weapon – a three-pronged spear that can cause untold destruction. It's the weapon of choice of the sea god Poseidon (and his Roman equivalent Neptune), and in Hindu mythology the god of destruction, Shiva, also carries a trident.

MYTHQUOTED

'From his weapons on the open road, no man should step one pace away.'

Odin, *Hávamál*

The Gods of Egypt #2

In a fight between Odin, Zeus, Ra, Ahura Mazda, Brahma – and anyone else who cares to join in – there could be only one winner. He might get a few bruises from Odin, and be slightly burned by Zeus' lightning bolts, but Ra, the Sun god of ancient Egypt, would triumph victorious.

Ra, the Sun god, was always depicted in hieroglyphs with a golden orb above his head.

Ra Checklist

★ The most important deity in Egyptian mythology, the Sun god Ra was the supreme power in the Universe, the god of creation and the Sun.

★ As the Sun god, it was Ra's job to ride across the sky in a golden ship, bringing light and warmth to every living creature.

★ Every night, for 12 hours, Ra was swallowed by the sky goddess Nut, before being reborn each morning at sunrise.

★ Ra had the head of a hawk and the body of a human.

★ According to some Egyptian creation myths, Ra emerged from the primeval waters of Chaos and 'spat out' the gods Tefnut (moisture) and Shu (air).

★ According to some myths, when Ra saw the perfection of all the beauty in the world, he cried. The tears fell to Earth and grew into human beings.

Osiris Checklist

☆ Osiris was a wise king who was married to his sister Isis.

☆ He was the father of Horus, also a king of Egypt.

☆ Osiris became the king of the dead and the judge of the Underworld. Every pharaoh would become Osiris after death, after being the embodiment of Horus when alive.

☆ Osiris was also the god of vegetation. He was often painted with green skin in hieroglyphs, symbolising renewal and growth.

Isis Checklist

☆ Isis was the ultimate goddess for she was the mother of Horus and both wife and sister of Osiris.

☆ When Osiris was murdered (by their brother Seth), Isis collected the parts of his dismembered body and put them back together with bandages – starting the tradition of the ancient Egyptian practice of mummifying the dead.

☆ She brought Osiris back to life, a process that introduced the concept of resurrection for the first time. This later had a profound influence on other religions, including Christianity.

☆ Isis was also worshipped as goddess of fertility. She was often painted with a female body and cow's head!

The Egyptian number for one million was a hieroglyph of a god with his arms raised in the air.

Amun Checklist

☆ Amun was worshipped as the king of the gods. He was shown in human form, with two plumes on his head.

☆ Amun was later merged with Ra into Amun-Ra, becoming the most famous of all the gods throughout ancient Egypt.

The Olympians

When it comes to who stands on the top of the podium at the Mythology Olympics, there can be only one group of gods and goddesses who deserve to take the gold medal, beating their defeated parents, the Titans, who take silver (see page 24). It is, of course, the legendary Olympians.

How Many Can You Remember?

These are the 12 Olympian gods. Look at the list below for 30 seconds. Then look away and try to write down as many of the names as you can remember. If you get all 12, give yourself a pat on the back!

Zeus Checklist

Zeus overthrew his father, the Titan, Cronus.

He won a draw with his brothers and became the supreme ruler of the gods.

Zeus is lord of the sky. The name Zeus means 'bright' or 'sky'.

His weapon is a thunderbolt, which he throws at those who displease him. The bolts were built for him by the Cyclopes giants.

He's referred to as the 'Father of Gods and Men'.

Poseidon Checklist

Poseidon is the brother of Zeus.

He is the lord of the sea, earthquakes and horses.

His name is Greek for 'husband'.

His weapon is a trident, which when used would shake the Earth, and shatter any object.

He is second only to Zeus in power among the gods.

Poseidon and Medusa created the magical flying horse, Pegasus.

Ares Checklist

Ares is the son of Zeus and Hera. He was disliked by both parents.

He is the god of war, and represents violence, but is considered a coward.

The Amazons, giant warrior women, were his daughters. Their mother was a peace-loving nymph named Harmony.

Ares and Aphrodite had a daughter, Harmonia, goddess of harmony.

Ares was never very popular – either with men or the other Immortals. As a result, he is not worshipped as much as other gods.

Hermes Checklist

Hermes is the son of Zeus and Maia.

He is the god of trade, sport, athletes and eloquence.

He is Zeus' messenger. He is the fastest of the gods.

He wears winged sandals, a winged hat, and carries a magic wand.

Hermes was born in a cave on a mountain in Arcadia; he was conceived and born within the course of one day.

Apollo Checklist

Apollo is the son of Zeus and Leto.

He is the god of music, often seen playing a golden lyre, and light. He also taught man medicine.

One of Apollo's more important jobs was to drive the Sun across the sky, using his chariot with four horses.

He has an athletic appearance – unlike the other Olympians.

According to Homer's *Iliad*, Apollo helped Paris kill the Greek hero Achilles in the Trojan War.

The Man, the Myth, the Legend: Robin Hood!

No one has ever been able to prove that Robin Hood, perhaps the most legendary character of medieval Britain, ever existed. Hood, like the tales of his heroics, has grown in stature over the centuries; his stories of robbin' the rich and giving to the poor, and fighting off the dastardly Prince John, are as epic as any heroic archetype in mythology. But what do we really know about him?

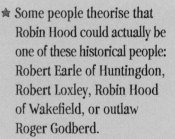

The Legend Checklist

★ Robin Hood was a legendary bandit who roamed medieval England in the 12th century, stealing from the rich, helping the poor.

★ He was the best archer and swordsman of the time.

★ The stories about Robin appealed to the common people of England because he stood up against those in power who had all the money.

★ Some people theorise that Robin Hood could actually be one of these historical people: Robert Earle of Huntingdon, Robert Loxley, Robin Hood of Wakefield, or outlaw Roger Godberd.

★ Academics trying to find the 'real' Robin Hood have a problem – the names 'Robin' and 'Hood' were fairly common back then.

The Myth Checklist

☆ A character called Robin Hood appears in five early ballads, dating from around 1450–1500.

☆ The earliest known mention of Robin Hood is in William Langland's 1377 writing called *Piers Plowman*.

☆ There was no mention of Maid Marion or Friar Tuck in the early ballads.

☆ Little John, Much the Miller's Son and William Scarlok (not Scarlet), are the only Merry Men mentioned in the early ballads.

☆ We still have no idea why Robin Hood is an outlaw, and what 'crime' he committed to be given that title!

The Man Checklist

★ A source of the legend may lie in an old French custom of celebrating 1 May, May Day.

★ A character called Robin des Bois, or Robin of the Woods, was associated with this spring festival and may have been transplanted to England – with a slight name change.

★ Stories of Robin Hood first appeared in many locations around England, including Barnsdale in Yorkshire and Sherwood Forest in Nottinghamshire.

★ In the 13th century, new laws were passed that stopped ordinary people from hunting freely in forests, land now claimed as the property of kings and nobles. Because of these laws, plus high taxes and the Black Death that killed millions of poor people, there was much social unrest. This finally led to an event called the Peasants' Revolt of 1381 where the common man rose up and revolted against the nobleman. Robin Hood is a personification of the turmoil that ordinary people of England were experiencing at that time. He may have been real once … but no one can prove it!

Here Be Monsters #3

CERBERUS

Here's a handy acronym to help you remember about Greek mythology's most fearsome three-headed dog-monster.

C erberus, the dog, is a monster with three heads.

E chidna, his mother, and Typhon, his father, were both monsters.

R esembles them both, with a serpent's mane and a dragon-like tail.

B ound to the land of the dead, he guards the River Styx …

E ating souls that escape and tormenting the rest for kicks.

R easonable men stay away for he craves living flesh.

U nder the domain of Hades, he remains vicious and blood-thirsty, never to be tamed.

S truggling with Hercules, his saliva sprouted a poisonous plant called aconite.

PHOENIX

The phoenix is a legendary bird with golden feathers that flew in the imaginations of Greek, Roman, Chinese, Japanese and Egyptian mythology. The size of an eagle, the phoenix hums a tune of mesmerising beauty, and according to legend lived for 500 years or more before dying and then famously being reborn.

Before its death, the phoenix built a nest of fragrant herbs and spices. Then it set the nest on fire and died in the flames, only for a new phoenix to rise from the ashes. The phoenix was associated with immortality and eternal rebirth in Egypt, and the Romans used it on coins to symbolise Rome, the Eternal City.

FENRIR

Fenrir, a monstrous wolf, was one of three terrible children of the Norse trickster god Loki. When Loki's other children were thrown out of Asgard, the home of the gods (see page 110), Fenrir was tied up with a magic chain that would restrain him. A silky but super-strong ribbon called Gleipnir was made out of some fairly strange ingredients, but it did the trick!

MYTHQUOTED

'It is sacred to the Sun, and different to other birds in the colours of its feathers and the nature of its beak. The general tradition says it lived 500 years.'

Tactitus, a Roman historian

Spirits in the Sky

Thousands of years before the first Europeans sailed their ships across the Atlantic Ocean to the New World, North America had its own creation myths ...

Earth, Wind and Fire

The Native American peoples of North America do not share a single unified system of mythology that tells them who they are or their beliefs about the creation of the world. For thousands of years, across more than 1,500 tribes (and many millions of people), the Native American mythology of creation was passed down through generations, evolving and changing with time, and within each tribe. The many different tribal groups each developed their own stories about the creation of the world, the appearance of the first humans, the place of humans in the Universe, and the roles of their own deities and heroes. Detailed inside every myth is the idea that spiritual forces, like an omniscient god, can be found throughout the natural world, in elements such as weather, fire, earth, water, wind, plants, animals and even the clouds. Many stories explain how the actions of certain ancestors, and the spirits of those ancestors, gave the Earth its present form.

The Great Spirit

The main deity in Native American mythology is the belief in a Great Spirit, a spiritual connection to the Earth and with one's ancestors. Like going to church on Sunday, Native American people worshipped their Great Spirit through traditions such as tribal dances and songs, notably the gruesome Sun Dance (Google it!). Alongside the Great Spirit, Father Sky, Mother Earth and Mother Corn are other important spirit forces. The Great Spirit is called many things by many tribes. To the Sioux and Algonquian peoples – two of the

The Hopi people's emergence creation myth is supercool. It spins the yarn of Spider Woman, a powerful Earth goddess and creator, who is the mother of life. Together with Tawa, the Sun god, Spider Woman sang the First Magic Song. This magic song brought the Earth, light and life into creation. Spider Woman then moved among humans, dividing them into the groups and races we know today.

biggest Native American tribes (and still going strong) – the Great Spirit was Wakan Tanka.

Wakan Tanka

So the legend goes, Waken Tanka placed all the stones and minerals in the ground, from which all life sprang, and plants grew wherever Tanka placed his hands in the ground. Every story in Native American mythology is an attempt to understand and connect with the Great Spirit, so that the world can be better understood.

Hybrids of Mythology #1

Part man, part creature, part totally awesome, these mythological creatures combine the physical features of human beings with creatures even uglier than you can ever imagine! The even more magical creatures forget about the human attributes altogether and join forces with other, even cooler, creatures from the animal kingdom ...

Half Man, Half Goat

Though perhaps not as cool as his half man, half horse cousin, the centaur, the often overlooked faun is just as popular as the satryr, his equivalent in Greek mythology, made famous by Aesop's fable, *The Satyr and the Traveller*.

With a man's torso and the lower body of a goat – and horns on his head! – the most famous of all modern fauns was Mr Tumnus who appeared in *The Lion, the Witch and the Wardrobe* by C.S. Lewis.

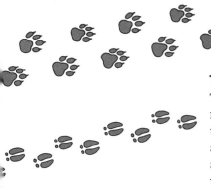

Centaur

Half man, half horse, centaurs are perhaps the most famous legendary hybrid creature, appearing in many ancient mythologies, as well as modern tales, such as the character of Oreius in the C.S. Lewis epic fantasy *The Lion, the Witch and the Wardrobe*. Sometimes depicted as noble creatures, often represented as brutal and aggressive, centaurs have the head, neck, chest and arms of a man and the body and legs of a horse.

The Riddle of the Sphinx

The legendary winged monster of Greek mythology that had a lion's body and a woman's head is known as the Sphinx (the Egyptian version traditionally has a man's head). As the legend goes, the Sphinx was sent to live on a rock outside the ancient city of Thebes as a punishment for some long-forgotten crime. Her presence on the rock scared the living daylights out of anyone who walked by. While living on the rock, the Sphinx was tasked with posing a riddle to any passerby: *'I have four legs in the morning, two legs at noon, and three legs in the evening, but I am weakest when I have the most legs. What am I?'*

When no one was able to solve the riddle, the Sphinx devoured them in one bite! It was Greek hero Oedipus who provided the correct answer: *'A human being walks on all fours as a baby, on two legs as an adult, and with a crutch as a third leg when he grows old.'*

After finally hearing the correct answer, the Sphinx killed herself.

Prometheus

If ancient Greek mythology is to be believed, then humankind has a lot to thank the Titan god Prometheus for. In mythology, Prometheus is known as a trickster, a rebel, a god who refused to obey the orders of Zeus, but he is also revered among the ancient Greeks as one of the most beloved of all the gods. For it was Prometheus who created mankind, stood up for us and gave us fire.

Prometheus created the first man, named Phaenon, out of clay and water. Unlike the animals on Earth, Prometheus created Phaenon to walk upright, just like the gods on Mount Olympus. Zeus disliked the human creatures Prometheus had created, but he could not uncreate them. Instead, Zeus confined them to the Earth and denied them immortality.

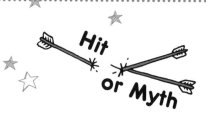

Hit or Myth

Prometheus was sometimes presented as a trickster. In a story called 'The Trick at Mecone' – a myth that teaches humans not to believe everything they see! – Prometheus tricks Zeus by asking him to choose between two food offerings: beef hidden inside an ox's stomach (something beautiful hidden inside something ugly) or bones wrapped in tasty fat (something ugly hidden inside something beautiful). Zeus chooses the fat bones and is disgusted!

Zeus is infuriated and asks Hephaestus, the god of blacksmiths, volcanoes and metallurgy, to create Pandora, the first woman, whose job is to bring the downfall of Prometheus' most precious creation …!

Prometheus Checklist

⭐ Prometheus, a Titan god of Greek mythology, was the god of fire.

⭐ He was credited with the creation of humankind and with giving them fire that he stole from Zeus.

⭐ The name Prometheus means 'forethought'.

⭐ Prometheus and his brother Epimetheus were charged with the task of populating the world, and providing humans with powerful, natural gifts.

⭐ Prometheus named his creations on Earth 'man'.

⭐ Epimetheus, Prometheus' thoughtless and foolish brother, paid little attention and when creating the animals, gave them many powerful attributes instead of to man: powerful teeth and claws to lions and bears, wings to birds, and swift legs to horses.

⭐ No powerful attributes remained for Prometheus to give to man. Instead, Prometheus invented a new feature, called intelligence, and gave it to the human race, giving them superiority over the animals.

⭐ Zeus, angered that Prometheus had given fire to man, had him chained to a mountain.

⭐ Every day, Zeus sent an eagle to pick and chew on Prometheus' liver, and every night the liver would heal itself.

Here Be Monsters #4

The Manticore

In Persian legends the manticore is a creature similar to the Egyptian sphinx. This bizarre-looking mythological monster-hybrid has the body of a lion, a human head with three rows of sharp teeth like a shark, bat-like wings, a scorpion's tail and a voice as deep as a foghorn! It devours its prey in one bite. Indeed, in English, manticore means 'man eater'.

The Thunderbird

The Horned Serpents, the Avanyu, the Kokopelli, the Piasa Bird – there are many cool mythical creatures of Native American mythology to check out. But none of them are as cool as the Thunderbird. It's believed that the Thunderbird, a mega-sized powerful falcon, created thunder and clouds when it flapped its wings, could shoot lightning bolts out of its eyes and was the servant of the Great Spirit. If you lived in North America 2,000 years ago, it was your daily job to not make the Thunderbird angry by living a good life.

The Yeti

The Yeti, also known as the Abominable Snowman, is a HUGE ape-like cryptid (an animal who some believe to exist, but no evidence confirms it) that is said to live in the Himalayan mountains, near Nepal and Tibet. Legend suggests he is 10ft (3m) tall, and looks like a cross between a polar bear and Chewbacca. The Yeti is probably the most famous creature of cryptozoology and is considered the brother-from-another-mother of the Bigfoot myth of North America.

FOOTPRINTS OF PROOF

In 1953, Sir Edmund Hillary and Tenzing Norgay – the first humans in recorded history to ascend to the top of Mount Everest – reported seeing large footprints in the snow while on their journey upwards. Though they never saw the beast, who did these footprints belong to?

YETI FACT FILE
Height 10ft (3m) plus
Weight Big and fat
Home Himalayan mountains
Colour White
Identifying features Large footprints

Magical Places #1

From the ancient Greek's Elysian Fields to Xibalba in Mayan legend, there are many magical kingdoms, realms and resting places in the world's greatest mythologies, many of whose locations still remain a puzzle for us to solve.

The Land beyond the Pillars

One of the biggest unresolved mysteries that gets the chins of archeologists all scratchy is also one of the strangest: where on earth is the sunken civilisation of Atlantis? Why did it disappear? And DID IT EVER EXIST?

According to *The Dialogues of Plato*, the Socratic stories of the famed Greek philosopher Plato, written in 370BC, this infamous continent under the sea is located somewhere in the Atlantic Ocean.

Often idealised as an advanced, utopian society full of very wise, alien-like superhumans, Atlantis – built by Poseidon, god of the sea, when he fell in love with Cleito, a mortal woman – has become famed in popular culture as a paradise where powerful Atlantians rule over Athenians (regular people from Athens, Greece) to try and make the world more peaceful and organised.

Beimeni
Home to the Fountain of Youth?

Shangri-La
Himalayan idyll

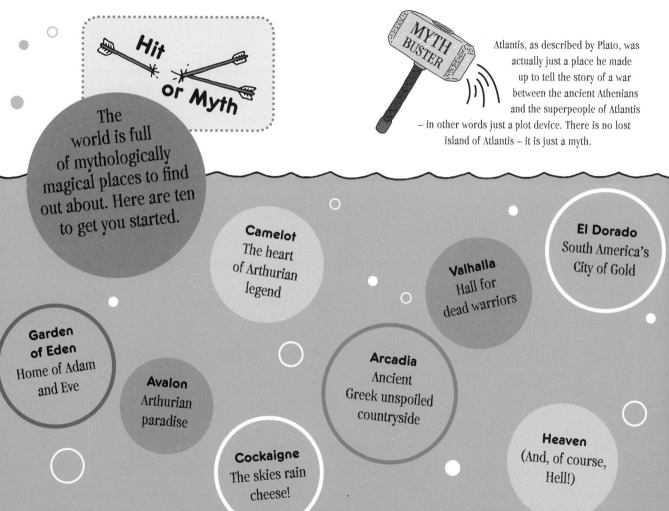

Hit or Myth

The world is full of mythologically magical places to find out about. Here are ten to get you started.

MYTH BUSTER

Atlantis, as described by Plato, was actually just a place he made up to tell the story of a war between the ancient Athenians and the superpeople of Atlantis – in other words just a plot device. There is no lost island of Atlantis – it is just a myth.

Camelot
The heart of Arthurian legend

Valhalla
Hall for dead warriors

El Dorado
South America's City of Gold

Garden of Eden
Home of Adam and Eve

Avalon
Arthurian paradise

Arcadia
Ancient Greek unspoiled countryside

Cockaigne
The skies rain cheese!

Heaven
(And, of course, Hell!)

The Princes of Persia

Almost 3,000 years ago, in what is now Iran, existed a place called Persia, and for centuries it was the home of the Persian Empire, a powerful dynasty that stretched from Europe to India. Out of this empire an epic mythology was born, and the fight between good and evil has been battling it out ever since ...

Following the reign of Zoroastrianism, Persia changed its belief to Islam.

The Persian Empire

The Persian Empire was founded by Cyrus the Great, around 550BC. Mr Great then went on to conquer Mesopotamia, Egypt, Israel and Turkey, making it, at the time, the largest empire on Earth! Cyrus allowed the peoples he conquered to keep their customs and religions, as long as they paid their taxes and obeyed him. However, the Persian Empire, in general, practised the teaching of the prophet (a person who believes he can speak with God) Zoroaster. This was called Zoroastrianism and the supreme 'good god' that everyone worshipped was called Ahura Mazda.

Ahura Mazda

Angra Mainyu

Mythnomer

It was the Persians who developed, and made fashionable, the concept of 'Paradise' – a place where everything is, well, paradise! The English word 'paradise' comes from the Old Iranian word, *paridayda*.

Zoroastrianism

A thousand years after Persian mythology first developed, around 1500BC, Zoroastrianism emerged. The religion held on to many previous mythological beliefs, but added new themes, deities and myths. The result was a mythology based on a cosmic conflict between good and evil! Two powerful gods, and twin brothers, Ahura Mazda (the creator, a god of light, truth and goodness) and Angra Mainyu (spirit of darkness, lies, evil, destruction, disease and demons), were constantly at war. The world was their battlefield. They were equally matched, but the eventual winner would be crowned God Almighty. To help Ahura Mazda win this battle, he had a band of angels, called the Yazatas, and good spirits, called ashavans. For those who believe in Zoroastrianism, the battle between good and evil still rages.

Mithra is the Persian divine spirit who keeps watch over the world. Born of a virgin mother on 25 December, he is often described as the inspiration for Jesus Christ.

Hit or Myth

Zoroastrianism is believed to have had a major influence on the Jewish/Christian and Islamic faiths, with theological historians believing that those religions initially developed from Persian traditions.

Hybrids of Mythology #2

Griffin

With the body of a lion, head and wings of an eagle, and the tail of a serpent, the griffin was a creature that appeared in Greek mythology. Because it combined an eagle and a lion, the griffin represented mastery of the sky and the Earth and became associated with strength and wisdom. Famously, griffins pulled the chariots of Zeus and Apollo.

Minotaur

The Minotaur was a monstrous creature with the head of a bull on a man's body – and it loved to gorge itself on human flesh. According to one of the most famous Minotaur tales in Greek mythology, this hybrid creature was the offspring of King Minos' wife and a bull. The king kept the Minotaur locked up in a labyrinth; every nine years, seven young men and maidens from Athens were sacrificed to the Minotaur. One year, the Athenian hero, Theseus, decided that this slaughter must stop and that he would be the hero that would slay the beast. King Minos' beautiful daughter, Ariadne, agreed to help the handsome hero and gave Theseus a thread to help him retrace his steps out of the maze. Our hero killed the Minotaur with his bare hands, then calmly walked out of the maze, simply following Ariadne's special thread!

Ammut

In ancient Egyptian mythology, the Underworld demon Ammut was the most terrifying of all creatures – her head was that of a crocodile, her body was a lion at the top and a hippopotamus at the bottom. Known as 'the Devourer', Ammut was the creature that ancient Egyptians feared the most.

HOOOOOOOOOOOOOOOOOWL

Berserkers

Berserkers are wild warriors of Norse mythology, and are half man, half bear. The word 'berserk' means 'bare-of-shirt', meaning someone who doesn't wear armour! Berserkers are believed to be the origin of the werewolf legend, changing from bears to wolves as the legends of berserkers become popular. According to the myths, a berserker's howl had extraordinary strength and neither iron nor fire could hurt them. However, when not fighting, berserkers often went wild, giving us the popular phrase in the English language – 'going berserk'.

What's Inside the Box?

In ancient Greek mythology, Pandora was the first woman to be created. Her role was to bring about the downfall of humankind by opening up her box of evil – Pandora's Box. This myth – often regarded as a metaphor for humanity's curiosity – has endured for thousands of years for one simple reason: we all want to know what's inside the box.

Hit or Myth

Throughout history, as the myth of Pandora's Box has been analysed by historians in cardigans, similarities have been noted between Pandora and Eve, the first female creation as detailed in the book of Genesis in the Bible. Like Pandora, Eve was the first woman, and she too was responsible for unleashing destruction to an innocent, all-male Paradise when she ate the apple, after being tempted by the serpent.

MYTH BUSTER

Though the myth is called Pandora's Box, historians believe that it is more likely to have been a large jar than a box. But Pandora's Large Jar doesn't quite have the same ring to it!

What the Box Means

The meaning of this myth has puzzled historians for centuries. The conclusion many have come to is that when Pandora traps Hope in the box she was saving Hope for mankind. But some believe Pandora – by trapping Hope in the box, instead of letting it fly out – was keeping Hope away from humanity. The 19th-century philosopher Friedrich Nietzsche assumed the worst: 'By saving Hope for humanity, Pandora doomed us all to suffering in vain.'

Pandora Checklist

☆ Pandora was the first woman, created in clay by Hephaestus, the Titan god of metallurgy.

☆ Athena gave life to Pandora, Aphrodite made her beautiful and Hermes taught her to be cunning and deceitful.

☆ Zeus sent Pandora as a gift to Prometheus' foolish brother Epimetheus, who married Pandora, despite warnings from Prometheus not to accept any gift from Zeus.

☆ Pandora brought to Earth with her a box, though she did not know what was inside it. When Pandora opened the box, she released war, old age, evil, disease, poverty, famine and all the other troubles now known to mankind into the world, and Zeus thus gained his revenge on the human race!

☆ When Pandora opened the box, the troubles flew out into the world, leaving only Hope at the bottom, the last remaining item to give comfort to mankind.

Myths That Exist?

Myths are part of our everyday lives, whether we are putting teeth under our pillows for the Tooth Fairy, or travelling to Scotland to spot the Loch Ness Monster.

Do You Believe in Fairytales?

Fairies, and fairytales, come in all shapes and sizes, and can be seen in one shape or form in many cultures around the world. From gentle household fairies to the Tooth Fairy who takes away teeth that have fallen out (for a price, of course), through to the Fairy Godmother of fairytales such as Cinderella, and the folktales of Islam's Arabian Nights, such as Aladdin. Fairies are everywhere! Are they fallen angels often seen as luminescent females with pointy ears and magical wands, or are they mythological personifications of natural light phenomena? Elves, fairies, sprites, pixies, nixies – they can be called different things, depending on the fairytale!

Loch Ness Monster

The Loch Ness Monster, or Nessie, is a legendary lake monster (though no proof of its monstrousness exists) associated with Loch Ness, the largest and deepest lake in Scotland. Legends about the monster have been told for centuries.

The first reported sighting was made in 565AD by St Columba, an Irish missionary who had come to Scotland to spread Christianity. According to legend, Columba stopped the monster from attacking a man by making the sign of the cross and ordering the beast to leave.

The Loch Ness Monster is not just a beast from medieval mythology, however.

A number of people have reported sighting Nessie in modern times, most famously in 1933, and generally describe the creature as about 30ft (9.1m) in length, with a long neck and flippers in the middle of its body – a description that matches that of a dinosaur called a plesiosaur.

In 1987 Operation Deepscan became the most expensive search for a mythological monster to date, costing more than £1 million. The operation involved a boat searching the entire loch with sonar. They didn't find Nessie but they did receive three sonar 'pings', which were, according to those on board, 'larger than a shark but smaller than a whale'. What on earth could that have been?

LOCH NESS MONSTER FACT FILE
Height Unknown
Weight Unknown
Home Loch Ness, Scotland
Colour Unknown
Identifying features Long neck, flippers
Goes by the name of Nessie

The Hindu Times

For well over 4,000 years, Hinduism has remained one of the main global religions. Over this time, thousands of sacred stories and heroic epics that make up the mythology of Hinduism, including Ayyavazhi, Tamil and Buddhism, have permeated Indian culture, turning it into one of the richest mythologies in the world.

Hindu Deities

Brahma-rama

Hindus believe there is only one true god, a supreme spirit called Brahma. All Hindus believe that Brahma is present in every person as the eternal spirit or soul, called the atman, and most Hindus have a personal god or goddess, such as Shiva, Krishna or Lakshmi, which they worship every day. These are lesser gods and goddesses.

Brahma	Creator god
Parvati	Goddess wife of Shiva, both compassionate and ferocious
Ganesha	God of good fortune and wisdom
Indra	God of storms and rain
Shiva	God of vengeance and destruction
Varuna	God and ruler of the sky; later became god of water
Vishnu	Preserver god and protector of life

Incarnation

One of Hindu mythology's key beliefs is reincarnation (sometimes called the transmigration of souls): when you die your soul is born again into a new living body.

It's Time to Diwali

Diwali, or Deepavali, is the largest and most ancient of all religious festivals in India and is seen as the beginning of a new year. Celebrated by Hindus around the world, usually in October, Diwali remembers the coronation of the god-king Rama, after his epic mythological battle with Ravana, the Demon King of Lanka. The war symbolises the eternal battle between good and evil in Hindu mythology. Diwali, the 'row of lights', signifies the victory of light over darkness, knowledge over ignorance and hope over despair. Hindus celebrate Diwali by lighting oil lamps, setting off firecrackers, decorating their homes and offering prayers to the Hindu gods, Sita and Rama, Radha and Krishna, Lakshmi, the goddess of wealth, and Ganesha.

Ganesha says Shubh Diwali – Happy Diwali!

Depicted with an elephant's head on a human body, Ganesha is perhaps the most popular god of all Hindu mythology.

MYTHQUOTED

The two great Hindu epics, the Mahabharata and the Ramayana, written sometime between 300BC and 300AD, contain stories about a number of major deities. After that time, Hindu mythology and religion was continued in the Puranas, sacred texts of stories of the old days.

Do You Believe in Magic?

Magic and supernatural powers go hand in hand with witches and wizards, along with wands, broomsticks and other pointy things. People, or supernatural beings, thought to possess magical powers or to command supernatural forces, can be called many names – witch, wizard, warlock, sorcerer, enchanter, necromancer, shaman, conjuror, diviner.

Morgan le Fay

Morgan le Fay, from the British Arthurian legends, is the wicked enchantress who constantly tries to combat, and trick Arthur's wizard-friend Merlin, her bitter rival, with her spells. Morgan is always on the lookout to overthrow King Arthur, destroy Camelot and kill the Knights of the Round Table.

Merlin

Merlin, a powerful wizard who was the companion and advisor of King Arthur throughout his life, is perhaps the most famous wizard of all time. The original myth was based on a popular magician named Myrddin, who first appeared in Celtic mythology in the Middle Ages. The classic depiction of Merlin that we all know and love first appears in the *Historia Regum Britanniae*, written in around 1136. In these writings, Merlin is based on a mixture of historical and legendary figures.

Circe

In Homer's *Odyssey*, the famous epic poem of ancient Greece, the hero Odysseus met a witch named Circe. Circe had the power to turn people into animals and monsters! Her island home was populated with lions, bears and wolves – all humans who had been transformed by her wicked magic. Although she was able to transform many of Odysseus' men into pigs, the hero had a special herb that protected him from her spells.

Real World Witch-Hunt

During the Middle Ages in Europe – around 1,000 years ago – the belief in the existence of witches was very common. Witches were believed to be worshippers of the Devil, and thousands of women across the continent were executed after being accused of witchcraft. They were burned alive on top of a flaming pyre to rid the body of evil demons. During the mass migration of English people to North America in the 17th century, people took their fear of witches with them to the New World. An infamous witch-hunt in Salem, Massachusetts, in 1692 resulted in the deaths of 19 women.

Mythnomer

Men who possess the powers associated with witchcraft are often known as wizards or warlocks. The word 'wizard' simply means 'wise one'.

The Epic of Gilgamesh

As relevant today as it was to the Sumerians of ancient Iraq 3,500 years ago, the *Epic of Gilgamesh* is the earliest work of literature ever discovered. It tells the life of a man who loses his friend to death, and embarks on a hero's quest for immortality.

MYTHQUOTED

On his travels, Gilgamesh meets a goddess who tries to persuade him to end his quest for immortality with these words:

Gilgamesh, whither rovest thou?
The life thou pursuest thou shalt not find.
When the gods created mankind,
Death for mankind they set aside,
Life in their own hands retaining.

Gilgamesh was a legend, a mythical Sumerian King of Uruk, though some historians believe him to be based on a historical figure – and a popular hero in the mythology of ancient Iraq.

Gilgamesh Checklist

★ The narrative theme is Gilgamesh's quest for fame, glory and immortality through heroic deeds.

★ The best-known story detailed in the epic is the tale of a great flood. Many believe this to be the inspiration behind the story of Noah and the flood in the Bible.

★ It is a series of five poems from around 2100BC. The five were combined to make it epic!

★ The first half tells the story of Gilgamesh, King of Uruk, and Enkidu, a man created by the gods to oppose Gilgamesh.

★ After an initial battle, Gilgamesh and Enkidu become bosom friends.

★ When Enkidu dies, Gilgamesh goes on a quest of self-discovery to find the secret of eternal life.

★ Gilgamesh learns at the end of his quest that death is the end of existence.

The Most Epic of Epics!

The *Epic of Gilgamesh* explores what it means to be human. The central premise of the poem is this: how can we live, when we know we must die?

Hit or Myth

In October 2011, a clay tablet containing a missing chapter of the *Epic of Gilgamesh* was discovered when the Sulaymaniyah Museum in Iraq purchased a set of tablets from a smuggler, including the *Epic*.

MYTH BUSTER

The *Epic of Gilgamesh* was originally written on 12 clay tablets, in cuneiform script. Around two-thirds of this version have been recovered from the site of the ancient Assyrian city, Nineveh. The tablets came from the library of King Ashurbanipal, the last great King of Assyria, who reigned around 600BC.

Standing on the Shoulders of Giants

They may always be big and strong but giants play many roles in myth and legend. Some are evil monsters, doing the bidding of others; some are gentle and compassionate, but misunderstood; and some are just clumsy and stupid.

Finn MacCool

Mr MacCool is the hero of Irish legend, the biggest and strongest giant in all of Ireland. According to folklore, a Scottish giant named Angus wanted to fight Finn in a battle to prove who was strongest. Finn agreed, and built a path of rocks across the sea to Scotland in order to fight his foe, so creating the famous Giant's Causeway. On the way to Scotland, Finn heard that Angus was twice his size and got scared. But he came up with a cunning plan. On the day of the fight, Angus crossed the Causeway from Scotland and knocked on Finn's door. Finn's wife answered and told Angus that Finn had gone for walk. Angus heard a baby cry, went to take a look and found a giant baby in a cradle. 'If that's the size of Finn's baby, imagine the size of Finn!' he sobbed. He ran out the door, and back to Scotland. Little did he know that the baby was actually Finn in disguise!

Dressing as a baby can help you avoid fights!

size of an adult human

QUICK FACT

In Minnesota, USA, a 55ft (16.8m) statue of the Jolly Green Giant weighing 4 tons was created in 1978 when visitors to the USA's largest manufacturer of sweetcorn and peas kept asking where they could find the giant they saw on the tins.

Mythnomer

The word 'giant' comes from the Greek *gigantes* (meaning 'earthborn'). In Greek mythology, the Cyclopes were a group of one-eyed giants. Their single eye (a big one!) was located in the middle of the forehead. It was the Cyclopes that gave Olympian god Zeus the ability to throw lightning bolts.

Hit or Myth

In Native American mythology of the Lakota people, Waziya is a giant who is responsible for blowing the winter wind.

Giants of Jotunheim

Giants, or Jotnar, run amok all over Norse mythology. There are thousands of them – from the frost giants of Jotunheim, the giants' realm (where they all live in a huge castle called Utgard), to the fire giants of Muspelheim. The main source of evil and mischief, they create havoc and destruction for the gods. In Ragnarok (see page 110), the fire giants of Muspelheim play a major role in the apocalypse!

Persephone and the Pomegranate Seed

In ancient Greek mythology, the tricky-to-pronounce Persephone was the beautiful goddess of fertility, daughter of Zeus and Demeter, the goddess of agriculture. The Romans loved her as Proserpina, but when Persephone married Hades, and became queen of the Underworld, her life took a strange turn for the worst ...

Persephone is pronounced as 'Per-seph-er-nee' and not 'Percy-phone' as you might think!

The Four Seasons

Persephone's most famous myth became an allegory used to explain the cycle of the four seasons: winter, spring, summer and autumn. To the ancient Greeks, it was a mystery why, for some parts of the year, their lands were covered with growing plants, and at other times the plants were dead, only to be reborn when it warmed up. To account for this mystery, the ancient Greeks devised a story about Persephone and a pomegranate seed.

Naughty Hades

Hades, the god of the Underworld in Greek mythology, appears in very few myths. But the one he is most famous for is the kidnapping of Persephone. He saw the beautiful Persephone one day, while riding his chariot on Earth, and fell immediately in love with her. Hades asked Zeus for permission to marry Persephone, but her mum, Demeter, would never agree. So, being the good father Zeus wasn't, he agreed to help Hades kidnap Persephone. While picking flowers one day, Persephone reached down for a fragrant blossom … but instead of picking it, the world collapsed and swallowed her whole. Hades emerged in a chariot, grabbed Persephone, and swiftly took her to the Underworld. When Demeter discovered that her daughter was missing, she searched all over, causing drought and devastation wherever she went on Earth.

Fearing the consequences of Demeter's anger, Zeus alerted Hades that Persephone must be returned to her mother. Before letting her go, however, Hades gave Persephone a pomegranate to eat. Persephone ate the fruit, without realising that anyone who ate food in the kingdom of the dead must remain there for eternity. Hades – you trickster!

In the end, Zeus and Hades came to an agreement: Persephone would spend part of every year with her mother, and part with Hades in the Underworld. When Persephone is with her mother the Earth is fruitful, but when she is with Hades Demeter mourns her daughter's absence and lets the land lie lifeless and without crops.

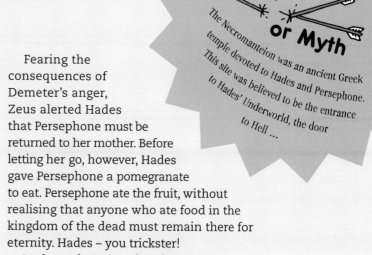

Hit or Myth

The Necromanteion was an ancient Greek temple devoted to Hades and Persephone. This site was believed to be the entrance to Hades' Underworld, the door to Hell …

Norse Superheroes

ODIN

Aka Chief of the warrior gods.
Special power Has a throne called Lidskialf, from which he can see anything happening in the Universe.
Likes Disguising himself as a traveller and wandering undetected through the world of humans.
Sidekicks Two pet ravens, Hugin and Munin, who fly through the Universe and bring back news.

THOR

Aka God of thunder.
Special power Has a throwing hammer, Mjolnir, which never misses its target, and has the power to restore life to the dead. Also wears a belt, Meginjardir, which doubles his superhuman strength.
Did you know? Thursday is named after Thor in many languages.
Sidekicks A pair of goats, Tanngniost and Tanngrisni, that pull Thor's chariot across the sky.

LOKI

Aka Trickster god who eventually turned evil.
Special power Shape-shifting.
Weird fact Loki gave birth to a horse called Sleipsir after shape-shifting into a mare.
Sidekick Loki once partnered up with Thor to win back his hammer from a giant who had stolen it. They disguised themselves as a bride and groom.

FREYA

Aka Goddess of love.
Special power She has a feather coat that gives the wearer the power of flight. Freya also possesses the beautiful Brising necklace, which was cursed – the result of trickery by the black dwarves.
Mode of transport A chariot pulled by two large cats.
Sidekick The boar Hidisvini, who is always by her side.

The Myths of the Living Dead

Despite being a very old mythological phenomenon – dating back almost a thousand years – vampire myths and legends are still all the rage in the 21st century.

According to Legend ...

In European folklore, a vampire is a living corpse that rises from the grave and sucks the warm blood from the bodies of the living. Should you be bitten by a vampire, you will turn into a vampire too.

Vampire Checklist

★ A vampire is cold to the touch.

★ A vampire's body does not decay like a normal corpse.

★ Vampires leave their graves every night in search of victims and their blood.

★ Vampires must avoid sunlight.

★ Vampires often sleep in their own coffins during the day.

Vlad the Impaler

In the history and legend of Eastern Europe, Dracula was the popular name of Vlad the Impaler, a merciless Romanian tyrant of the 1400s. Dracula means 'heir of the Order of the Dragon', dedicated to fighting the Turks.

Vlad was the prince of Walachia, a town near Transylvania, Romania. This cruel and fascinating man would supposedly impale his enemies on stakes around the dinner table so he could listen to their screams as he ate. He also had a reputation for roasting children, and is said to have killed over 100,000 people.

The legends of his cruel behaviour led to the association of the word 'Dracula' with inhuman actions and the myth started there. But it was with Bram Stoker's novel that the vampire myth took our throats by the jugular. Written in 1897, *Dracula* is the definitive vampire narrative. In the book, a centuries-old vampire of Transylvania feasts on human blood every night, while pursued by hunters out to stop his killings. If you want to know what happens in the end … you'll have to read the book!

The Blood Countess

More than a myth, an actual person of history, Countess Elizabeth Báthory de Ecsed (1560–1614) was a serial killer from a noble Hungarian family, perhaps the most prolific female murderer of all time. Báthory was accused of torturing and killing hundreds of women, perhaps as many as 650, between 1585 and 1610. Her reputation as 'The Blood Countess', a female Dracula, relate to her penchant for bathing in the blood of her many victims, in the belief it would help to retain her youthful looks.

How to Kill a Vampire

Vampires are almost immortal. But remember, they can only enter your house if you invite them in. So, should you be tricked into allowing them to enter, you'd better learn these six ways to kill a vampire … quick sharp!

1 Sunlight or bright light (a torch may suffice)
2 A wooden stake plunged directly into the heart (table legs might work)
3 Silver (mum's jewellery?)
4 Tear its head off (you're on your own here)
5 A big fire (set fire to the house and run away)
6 Garlic (always eat it for dinner, if you're expecting a vampire)

The King of Mischief

Everybody knows about Thor. You know, the guy with the hammer. The Norse god of thunder. He's pretty cool. But how much do you know about his adopted brother, Loki? This naughty Norse god is the king of mischief in mythology …

Loki arranged the death of Odin's beloved son Balder. One day, while the gods were tossing objects at Balder in fun, Loki – in an evil mood – tricked the blind Norse god Höd into touching Balder with mistletoe – the one thing that he knew could kill Balder.

Loki had several children, but they weren't human. With his second wife, the giantess Angrboda, Loki had three terrifying offspring: a supernatural being named Hel, a serpent named Jormungand and a wolf named Fenrir. As these creatures grew larger, Odin exiled them from Asgard. He cast Hel into the realm called Niflheim, where she became the goddess of the dead. Jormungand was thrown into the sea, and Fenrir was bound with magical chains and fastened to a huge rock.

Has a reputation for playing pranks and being a trickster, an archetype of mythology.

To punish Loki, the gods captured his sons, Narfi and Vali. They turned Vali into a wolf and let him tear his brother Narfi to pieces. They then took Narfi's intestines and used them to tie Loki to rocks in a cave where a poisonous serpent dripped venom onto him slowly – Loki's shouts of pain supposedly caused earthquakes here on Earth!

According to Norse legend Loki will remain in that cave until the end of the world, Ragnarok, arrives (see page 110). It is believed that during Ragnarok, Loki will be untied and lead the fire giants of Muspelheim against the gods, but will be killed in a fight with Heimdell.

The *Poetic Edda*, a 13th-century collection of Norse poems, contains one of the earliest references to Loki.

Loki is able to change his appearance and has been a fish, a horse, a fly and even an old lady!

Loki is the Norse god of fire.

Loki's father was not Odin – he was a giant and his mother may have been a giantess.

He lives in Asgard, the home of the Norse gods, and one of the Nine Worlds. Loki was a companion of Thor on many of his quests and adventures.

Magical Creatures #1

Evil creatures are one aspect of monster mythology. But magical creatures are another thing altogether!

Unicorn

The word 'unicorn' comes from the Latin for 'one-horned' and refers to an imaginary beast that appears in the legends of China, India, Mesopotamia (in the Middle East) and Europe. Since medieval times the unicorn has often been portrayed as a horse with a single horn growing from its forehead. Though descriptions of the animal differ between sources, they all agree on the horn. Some images of unicorns were probably based on real animals, such as the one-horned rhinoceros or the narwhal – a small whale with a single long tooth or tusk that resembles a spiral, ivory horn.

In Chinese tradition, the unicorn was one of four magical or spiritual creatures – along with the phoenix, tortoise and dragon – that were regarded as signs of good fortune. The appearance of a unicorn signalled the birth or death of a great person; one was said to have appeared when Confucius was born.

Sleipnir

In Norse mythology, Sleipnir is Odin's grey eight-legged horse, the offspring of Loki and the stallion Svaðilfari (from when Loki disguised himself as a mare!). Sleipnir's eight legs were said to represent the eight dimensions of heaven; he had prodigious strength and speed and was considered the best horse in the world. His name means 'gliding', so he presumably was a very smooth ride too.

MYTH BUSTER

Think you've found a genuine unicorn horn? Here are three ways to tell if it's real.

①

Take the horn and trace a circle on the floor with the tip. Place a spider in the circle. If the spider is unable to leave the circle, the horn is real.

Get a pot of cold water and
place the horn in the water.
If the water boils, the horn is real.

③

②

Find a sick animal,
such as a bird. Feed the
animal some ground-up
horn dust. If the animal
recovers immediately,
the horn is real.

Celtic Mythology

Arthurian, Scottish, Gaulish, Welsh and Irish are all cultures that are fused together to make up the enduring stories of Celtic mythology. And when it comes to adventure, heroism and romance, Celtic mythology can be as bewitching as any other!

I Am Legend

Once a powerful race of people who dominated most of Europe, the Celts were reduced to a few small tribes after the Roman invasions of Britain, beginning in 43AD. However, despite this invasion, Celtic mythology survived, thanks to the efforts of medieval Irish and Welsh monks who wrote down the tales.

Tales That Wag

The ancient Celts had an extensive mythology made up of hundreds of stories, but our knowledge of the gods, heroes and villains of Celtic mythology actually comes from the Romans, as the warrior Celts never wrote anything down. After all, if you pick up a pen, how do you hold a sword?

The Celts sacrificed weapons to the gods by throwing them into lakes, rivers and bogs – places they saw as special.

Celts in Kilts

The Celts were a group of people who spread throughout Europe 1,000 years before Jesus Christ – that's almost 3,000 years ago. They inhabited an area extending from the British Isles to Turkey. They had a reputation as strong and determined warriors and were respected by the Romans for their ferocious courage! But the Celts had their own gods too, many of whom they prayed to on the eve of a mighty battle with the Romans:

* **Brigit** Goddess of learning, healing and metalworking.
* **Dagda** God of life and death.
* **Danu** Fertility goddess and mother of the Tuatha Dé Danaan.
* **Epona** Goddess associated with fertility, water and death.
* **Lug** God of the Sun, war and healing.
* **Morrigan** Goddess of war and death.

MYTHQUOTED

Celtic mythology is associated with many symbols of nature: boars for courage and strength; fish for knowledge; serpents and dragons for trouble; birds for prophetic knowledge; and horses, cattle and pigs for fertility.

MYTH BUSTER

Magic and the supernatural played a significant role in Celtic mythology. Myrddin, a magician in Welsh tales, later became the famous wizard Merlin of Arthurian legend. Another common theme in Celtic mythology was the magic cauldron. It symbolised rebirth and its contents could bring fatally wounded warriors back to life again.

Goodness Gracious Goddesses

Mythology is not all about the men: some of the coolest myths are about goddesses, female deities and angelic characters. They may represent love, fertility or beauty, but they can kick butt too.

Goddess Checklist
There are thousands of goddesses of world mythology, far too many to name here. So let's get started on the Top Ten coolest. It's your job to learn about the rest!

#1 Aphrodite
The beautiful Greek goddess of love, beauty and fertility. Her name means 'raised from foam' as she was birthed from the crashing waves of a stormy sea. She was the child of Zeus and Dion and used a swan-drawn chariot to glide easily through the air.

#2 Arianrhod
The Celtic (Welsh) goddess of fertility and rebirth. She appears in the Mabinogion, one of the earliest written examples of prose literature in Britain, dating back to the 13th century.

#3 Artemis
An independent spirit, Artemis is the Greek goddess of hunting, nature and birth. Artemis was the daughter of Zeus and Leto, and twin sister of Apollo. A glorious white marble temple was built in her honour in Turkey, which became one of the 'Seven Wonders of the Ancient World'.

#4 Athena
Greek mythology's goddess of war and wisdom. She was the daughter of Zeus – she sprang from his head fully grown and clothed in armour!

#5 Bastet
The famous Egyptian cat goddess was the protector of cats and pregnant women. Domestic cats were revered in ancient Egypt and in the royal palaces cats were adorned with bejewelled collars and were even allowed to eat from the pharaoh's plate. More than 300,000 mummified cats were discovered when the temple of the cat goddess Bastet, at Per-Bast, was excavated in 1887.

#6 Ceres
The name of this Roman goddess of agriculture and grains comes from the old word root 'ker', meaning 'to grow'. In turn, Ceres has become the origin of our modern word, cereal.

#7 Ceridwen

An enchantress of the Moon, magic, agriculture, nature, poetry, language, music, art, science and astrology.

#8 Frigg

The Nordic goddess of marriage, childbirth, motherhood and wisdom is famous for her foreknowledge.

#9 Lakshmi

The Hindu goddess of purity and wealth, Lakshmi is commonly portrayed as a beautiful woman with four arms, standing on a lotus flower. It is during the famous festival of Diwali that Lakshmi is particularly worshipped.

#10 Venus

The Roman goddess of love and beauty. She appears in the tale 'Venus and the Queen', is the mother of Cupid (he of the arrow) and is one of the 12 Olympian gods.

As the eldest daughter of Zeus, the wicked Greek goddess Atë, is the personification of evil, misfortune, delusion, obsession, guilt, infatuation and mischief. Atë was known in ancient Greek myths as a goddess that would encourage and seduce men to behave in a way that would ultimately end in their death – teaching us all a moral not to be guided by our temptations. In William Shakespeare's play *Julius Caesar*, Atë is mentioned in one of the author's most famous lines:

'And Caesar's spirit, ranging for revenge,
With Atë by his side come hot from Hell,
Shall in these confines with a monarch's voice
Cry "Havoc!" and let slip the dogs of war ...'

Perseus and Medusa

In ancient Greece there was a cruel king called Polydectus who wanted to marry a woman called Danae. Danae had a brave son called Perseus, who was not fond of Polydectus. The king decided to send Perseus away on a dangerous quest, hoping that he would not return.

Medusa

Perseus' quest was to kill the Gorgon Medusa and bring back her head. Medusa was once a beautiful but vain girl. She made the mistake of boasting that she was the most beautiful girl in the land, better-looking than any goddess. The gods heard this and as punishment they turned her into a Gorgon – a monster with snakes for hair. Worst of all, anyone she laid eyes upon immediately turned to stone.

The Quest

Knowing that his quest was impossible, Perseus visited the Temple of Athena to pray for help. The gods heard his prayer and granted him five gifts. These were a helmet of invisibility, a sword, a shiny shield and a magic pouch. The final gift was a pair of winged sandals from Hermes, which gave Perseus the ability to fly.

Perseus flew to the cave where Medusa lived and bravely walked through the entrance. But how could he defeat a creature he could not look at? Perseus remembered his gifts from the gods and used his shield to look at Medusa's reflection. He shut his eyes, swung his sword, and with one swoop cut off Medusa's head. He placed it in the pouch and set off back to King Polydectus.

The king grabbed the head and, before Perseus could warn him, looked into the Gorgon's eyes, turning him to stone. Perseus had succeeded in his challenge and now his mother was safe.

Three's a Crowd

Medusa had two sisters, Stheno and Euryale, immortal Gorgons with the same hideous appearance as mortal Medusa. They were all daughters of Phorcys, a sea god, and his sister, Ceto. Today, Medusa's name is the one we remember because she's the only Gorgon that Homer speaks of in his works.

MYTH BUSTER

Medusa appears on the flag of Sicily. She has been depicted in paintings by many famous artists, including Picasso, Rubens and Caravaggio.

The Big Feet of Bigfoot

Bigfoot, or sasquatch as he
is more commonly known in
the USA, is a massive monkey
looking monster, or
ape-like cryptid if you prefer,
that is believed to reside
in the forests of
North America.

Monkey Madness

Usually described as a large, hairy, 'bipedal humanoid' (a monkey that can stand upright), there is footage of Bigfoot walking through a forest on YouTube, but this has been denounced as a hoax, or rather, 'a large man in a monkey suit'.

In the last two decades, scientists have discounted the existence of Bigfoot in North America and consider it to be a combination of folklore, misidentification and hoax, and because of the large numbers of victims the creature would require for breeding and feeding. Not to mention, there is no evidence of Bigfoot's poo anywhere, which means it either eats it or hides it.

BIGFOOT FACT FILE
Height 10ft (3m) plus
Weight 500lb (227kg) plus
Home Montana, Idaho, Wyoming
Colour Brown
Identifying features
Hairy, smelly

Another Giant of Mythology

Ladies and gents, this giant guy needs no introduction! It's Goliath!

Fighting against the Israelite army in the Valley of Elah, in Christian mythology, the 10ft (3m) tall Goliath challenged the soldiers to one-on-one combat. A man called David was the only one to accept the challenge, but he outwitted the giant by knocking him down with a stone hurled from his sling and then chopping off his head – good skills David!

Magical Places #2

The Bermuda Triangle

Located in the Atlantic Ocean (somewhere near Atlantis, perhaps!), the Bermuda Triangle is situated between Bermuda, Puerto Rico and Florida, and it covers an area of 440,000 miles (708,000km) of sea – HUGE! The Devil's Triangle, as it is also known, is an infamous place where strange, supernatural occurrences are believed to happen, where ships and planes disappear, and where massive sea monsters have been known to hide!

Sadly, with modern technology, the myth of the Bermuda Triangle has been put to rest. On average, four aircraft and 20 boats go missing every year in the Triangle, but as one of the most travelled shipping and trade lanes in the world, that is less than 1 per cent of all ships, so quite an insignificant figure. Bah.

Even now, archaeologists and scientists are still discovering magical landscapes from civilisations previously thought lost, most famously the Nazca Lines, Peru. In 2012, archaeologists found the fabled White City, 'The City of the Monkey God', hidden under the dense jungle canopies in Honduras. In 2015, the largest Neolithic site ever found was discovered in Britain, an underground site that contains over 90 large and puzzling stones, situated just 2 miles (3.2km) from Stonehenge.

Hit or Myth

The Bermuda Triangle's bad reputation started with Christopher Columbus. His captain's log for 8 October 1492, said that inside the Triangle the ship's compass had gone crazy.

I Write the Myths

So what about the writers who actually wrote the myths? Let's have a look at Homer, Ovid and Virgil – the greatest mythology writers of all time.

Homer Checklist

★ Homer's *Iliad* and *Odyssey* are the oldest works of literature ever known to humankind. We don't know exactly when these were written, but some historians believe it was around 700–800 BC.

★ Homer had a unique ability to give his characters, such as Achilles (in the *Iliad*), a tremendous amount of perspective.

★ Homer himself is possibly a myth! Did he ever exist? Or were the *Odyssey* and the *Iliad* woven together by generations of storytellers?

★ According to legend, Homer was a blind poet who wandered from place to place telling tales of legendary heroes, gods and goddesses.

★ The *Iliad* and the *Odyssey* are written in a type of verse called dactylic hexameter, a way of writing that has 18-syllable lines with the first of every three syllables accented.

Virgil Checklist

★ A Roman poet, Virgil was born in 70BC and died in 19BC.

★ Around 30BC Virgil began composing the *Aeneid*, an epic about the legendary hero Aeneas and the founding of Rome.

★ Virgil died before finishing the *Aeneid*, modelled on the *Iliad* and *Odyssey*, but Romans could see it was a masterpiece.

★ Like the Greek poems, the *Aeneid* features the Trojan War, a hero on a long and dangerous quest, and visions of hand-to-hand combat between heroic warriors.

★ Virgil first wrote the entire *Aeneid* in prose and then turned it into verse a few lines at a time.

★ On his deathbed, Virgil requested that the manuscript of the unfinished *Aeneid* be destroyed, but fortunately Emperor Augustus ignored Virgil's dying wishes and preserved the work.

Ovid Checklist

★ This Roman poet was born in 43BC and died in 17AD.

★ He was best known for his collection of myths and legends titled the *Metamorphoses*.

★ The *Metamorphoses* tells many of the ancient myths and legends of Greece, Rome and the Middle East. All the stories have a common theme: change, or 'metamorphosis'.

★ Characters in each of the tales undergo some sort of transformation into other forms, including animals, plants and stars. The changes usually come either as a reward for obeying or helping the gods, or as a punishment for disobeying or challenging them.

★ Ovid's writings had a direct and massive impact on William Shakespeare's plays, some 1,600 years later.

Magical Creatures #2

Chimera

According to Greek mythology, the Chimera was a terrible fire-breathing creature, made up of various different animals: typically a lion's body, the head of a goat rising from its back, and a tail that ended with a snake's head. The Chimera was a sibling of Cerberus and the Hydra (see pages 46 and 37). The Chimera was slain by the hero Bellerophon with the help of the winged horse Pegasus.

Typhon

There are gods, and there are monsters, but rarely are there gods that are also monsters. In Greek mythology, there is no god/monster as powerful, dangerous, and downright deadly as Typhon.

He is described in many different ways, varying slightly from legend to legend, but aggregating the most popular descriptions gives us this image of the beast:

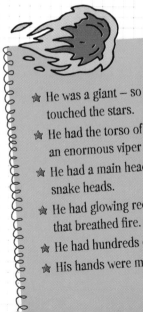

★ He was a giant – so tall his head touched the stars.

★ He had the torso of a man, but each leg was an enormous viper coil.

★ He had a main head that hosted 100 snake heads.

★ He had glowing red eyes and a 'savage jaw' that breathed fire.

★ He had hundreds of wings all over his body

★ His hands were made of 100 deadly serpents.

He sounds terrifying, and as if that all weren't bad enough, Typhon was not just a monster, he was also a god – the last child of Gaia (the Earth) and Tartarus (a violent and bottomless storm pit).

Being the fire-breathing monster he is, Typhon is believed to constantly struggle to become free, causing earthquakes and volcanic eruptions each time he moves.

Here Be Monsters #5

Balor the Deadly Giant

It wasn't just Greek mythology that featured Cyclops-esque monsters. In Celtic legends, Balor is often described as a giant with one large eye in his forehead, which killed everything in its sight with a poisonous beam of light when he opened it. Poor thing. Balor was once involved in a supernatural battle fighting for the Fomorians against the Tuathah Dé Danann. At the end of the battle, Balor commanded four men to pull up his huge eyelid … but as they did so, the hero of the Tuatha Dé Danann let fly a stone from his slingshot, hitting Balor smack in the eye. The stone went through the back of Balor's head, killing him instantly. With Balor dead, the Fomorians were defeated. The moral of this myth? Don't let a one-eyed giant fight for you – because their strength is also their weakness.

Grendel

Grendel is a gigantic monster, said to be descended from the biblical Cain (the first murderer, who slew his brother Abel). He appears in *Beowulf*, an Old English heroic epic poem set in Scandinavia, and one of the most important works of Anglo-Saxon literature. Dated between the 8th and early 11th century, it tells the story of how Beowulf, a great hero, comes to the aid of Hroðgar, the king of the Danes, by fighting a beast known as Grendel who has been terrorising the great hall built by Hroðgar and threatening the kingdom. Beowulf tears off Grendel's arm and kills him.

Leviathan

The Leviathan is arguably the best known sea-serpent legend in mythology. Originating in the Old Testament of the Bible, this immensely powerful creature's name has become synonymous with giant sea monsters ever since. In the Bible, Leviathan roamed the sea, breathing fire and spewing smoke from his nostrils and boiling the oceans with his hot breath.

Gods of the Far East

Enter the Dragon

In Western mythology, the dragon is feared as a fire-breathing monster who brings death and destruction. In the Far East, however, the dragon is revered as the supreme being of all animals and is the most important creature in Chinese mythology. For more than 2,000 years before Christ, a race of people known as the Xia dominated northern China. The Xia worshipped the snake, a creature that appears in some of the oldest Chinese myths. Over many centuries, the snake evolved into a dragon (or a four-legged snake), and it has since become one of the most enduring symbols of Chinese culture and mythology, representing power and excellence. In Chinese mythology there are nine classical types of dragon:

1 The Horned Dragon, or Lung, which can produce rain and is totally deaf.
2 The Winged Dragon.
3 The Earth Dragon, who controls rivers.
4 The T'ien Lung, or Celestial Dragon, who lives in the sky and guards the gods to keep them from falling out of the clouds.
5 The Spiritual Dragon, the Shen-lung, which generates wind and rain for the benefit of mankind.
6 The Dragon of Hidden Treasures, the Fu-tsang, guards hidden treasure or concealed wealth.
7 The Coiling Dragon, which lives in water.
8 The Yellow Dragon, which once emerged from water and presented the legendary Emperor Fu Shi with the elements of writing.
9 The Dragon King.

Mythnomer

The symbol for 'Dragon' in simplified Chinese is 龙.

Buddhism

The founder of Buddhism, Siddhartha Gautama, was an Indian prince who gave up his life of luxury to seek truth and wisdom. Once he found them, he became the Buddha, or 'the enlightened one'. Buddhists believe that humans are continually reborn into a new form of existence after death. If you've been good in this life, you'll return as a strong animal, such as a lion; if you've been bad, you'll be reincarnated as a worm, or slug! This is called karma. The ultimate goal of Buddhism is to escape reincarnation by achieving enlightenment and entering a timeless, heavenly state known as nirvana.

MYTH BUSTER

The dragon is one of the 12 animals of the Chinese zodiac, which assigns animals to years in the Chinese calendar. If you are born in the Year of the Dragon, you are very lucky indeed! The next Year of the Dragon is in 2024!

Dragons across cultures and mythologies in the Western regions of the world are often seen as fierce and destructive creatures. In the Far East, in countries such as China, dragons are viewed as powerful and enlightened.

Heavens Above

Cultures all around the world recognise that every life inevitably ends in death. Our bodies may decay, and out atoms may float away, but what, as many cultures ask, happens to our soul? Many cultures believe that the human spirit or soul continues to exist for eternity in some magical place ...

Heaven Is a Place on Earth

Mythologies throughout the millennia have set out a system of beliefs regarding an afterlife, a state of being that people enter when they die, or a magical place to which their souls, or spirits, go. Myths, legends and religious texts offer varying visions of the afterlife. These images reveal much about each culture's hopes and fears for the afterlife and often contain lessons about how people should live their lives.

Ancient Egyptian Afterlife

Ancient Egyptian mythology teaches us about the afterlife, where our bodies are transported to another world. They believed that the body had to be preserved after death in order for the human spirit to survive, and they went to great lengths to prepare the body for the afterlife. They built elaborate tombs to protect their most important dead and developed an elaborate form of mummification to keep the body from decomposing.

SEVEN STEPS TO MUMMIFICATION: DON'T TRY THIS AT HOME!

1 The body is washed and purified.
2 Organs are removed. Only the heart is left in the body.
3 The body is filled with stuffing.
4 The body is dried by covering it with a super-salty substance called natron.
5 After 50 days the stuffing is removed and replaced with linen or sawdust.
6 The body is wrapped in strands of linen and covered in a shroud.
7 The body is placed in a stone coffin called a sarcophagus. The mummy is ready for its journey to the afterlife.

Avalon

In Arthurian mythology, Avalon was a heaven on Earth, an island where harmony, health and good times ruled. When King Arthur was mortally wounded by Mordred in the Battle of Camlann, he was taken by boat to Avalon. It is believed Arthur will remain there until it is time for him to return to rule Britain again. We've not heard from him yet.

Valhalla

Valhalla, which means 'hall of the dead', was the great hall of the Norse god Odin. According to legend, the heroic warriors killed in the great battles of Norse mythology gathered in Valhalla, enjoyed the afterlife, with an unlimited supply of mead provided by a goat, and awaited Ragnarok, the end of the world. Valhalla has more than 640 doors, each one wide enough to allow hundreds of warriors to leave at the first sign of Ragnarok.

Elysium

Also called the Elysian Fields, in Greek and Roman mythology Elysium is the final resting place for the dead. Originally, only heroes whom the gods had made immortal went to Elysium, but over time it became the heavenly destination of anyone who had lived an honest and good life.

Better the Devil You Know

For every valiant hero doing his best on a quest to slay the dragon, or defeat a Minotaur, there is a devil, or demon, or all-round nasty piece of work – a pure personification of evil – that is hell-bent on standing in his way ...

The Personification of Evil

Virtually all religions, mythologies and cultures have different supernatural beings that are considered malevolent or even evil. These beings may simply be forces of nature, such as hurricanes, personified as the god of storms, for example.

In most mythologies a devil is a ruler among other evil spirits, who acts in direct opposition to the gods. If a god is light, a devil is dark. If an angel is good, then a demon is bad – 'Yin and Yang', to borrow a phrase from Chinese mythology.

The Devil

In the Christian mythology system, the Devil was, initially, a fallen angel who chose to become evil instead of worshipping God. Throughout the Middle Ages, it was part of the Christian belief that a separate devil existed for each of the seven deadly sins of humanity. Lucifer represented pride, Mammon greed, Asmodeus lust, Satan anger, Beelzebub gluttony, Leviathan envy, and Belphegor sloth. But, over the last few centuries, the myth has evolved ...

Iblis

Islam, the Muslim religion that was widely adopted in the Iranian–Persian Empire after Zoroastrianism (see pages 58 and 59) receded, has a devil being called Iblis, or Shaitan. Like Satan, he is a fallen angel. Iblis is in control of a demon army called shaitans, who tempt humans to sin.

The shaitans belong to a group of supernatural beings called djinni, the origin of the word 'genie'.

The Devil Fighting Belphegor

From Christian mythology, as detailed in The Book of Revelation, the demon Belphegor is one of the Seven Princes of Hell. This evil monster seduces humans on Earth into making a pact with the Devil, in exchange for mortal wealth and fame. The famous Number of the Beast, 666, is part of a prime number known as Belphegor's Prime. Whenever you see the number 666, it is believed that the Devil is nearby! Because of that, many superstitious people have a fear of the digits 6-6-6, a phobia known as hexakosioihexekontahexaphobia.

Banshee!

In Celtic folklore, *bean-sídhe*, or banshee, is the name of a female fairy that was usually a messenger of death. Her job: to transport you to Hell. If you saw a banshee, it meant that death was coming! With a wail that would pierce eardrums, and a physical appearance that would make you vomit, a banshee would often arrive at your house in a large black coach, pulled by headless horses, carrying a coffin.

Welcome to Hell

Hell. Helheim. Otherworld. Yomi. Underworld. Tartarus. Bagabo. Kazimu. Netherworld. Perdition. Xibalba. Land of the dead. Ukhu Pacha. Duat. House of Darkness. Annwn. O le nu'u-o-nonoa. Mictlan. Jahannam. Avici. Naraka. Diyu. No matter what the mythologies of the world call it, it's somewhere you never want to go!

It's Getting Hot in Here

The opposite of Heaven, Hell or the Underworld is one of the oldest concepts in most of the world's major mythologies. It came into existence at the same time as creation myths, when Chaos split into two – Heaven went up into the sky, Hell went deep underground. It's never the other way round, which suggests that all mythologies agree that's the way it should be. Let's take a look at some of the less well known, but still very cool, versions of Hell …

Grim Reaper

Lucifer

Anubis

Hit or Myth

In Islam, Jahannam is a place of blazing fire, boiling water, and a place where people who disobeyed God go.

Annwn

In Welsh mythology, the otherworld is often referred to as Annwn, roughly translated as 'not-world'. Primarily, the otherworld was the kingdom of the dead, and its hideous ruler was known as Arawn (Welsh). Celtic folklore is packed with legends of living rulers who entered Annwn. The magical King Arthur of Britain led an army – voluntarily – into the dark world to capture a magical cauldron. This story is recounted in the Book of Taliesin, dating back to 1350.

Xibalba

To the Mayan people of Mesoamerica, the Underworld was a very bad place indeed – and not one limited to very bad people, either. Heaven was reserved only for people who had died a violent death. Everyone else took an extended holiday to Xibalba, the Underworld, whose name means 'place of fright'. The Mayans believed that any cave or body of still water was a gateway to Xibalba.

MYTHQUOTED

Diyu, meaning 'earth prison', is the realm of the dead in Chinese mythology.

Mictlan

The Aztecs of Mexico believed that their Underworld consisted of eight layers, each with its own dangers, such as drowning or sharp blades. Souls descended through the layers until they reached Mictlan, the bottom-most part of the Underworld.

Yomi

The Underworld of Japanese mythology is Yomi, 'land of night or gloom'. This mystical location was empty until the creator goddess, Izanami, died after giving birth to the god of fire. The maggots that appeared in her dead body grew into a host of demons who populated Yomi and tormented the souls of the wicked. Yikes!

Not-So-Good Gods

Pluto

⭐ In Roman mythology, Pluto was the ruler of the underworld, the equivalent of the Greek Hades.

⭐ He's the son of Saturn, the equivalent of Cronus.

⭐ Pluto's weapon, in some classical depictions, was a two-pronged staff, called a bident. It would later become the weapon of choice of Satan, the devil in Christian mythology.

Coolness 10/10

Zeus

⭐ Zeus is the 'father of all men and all gods' in ancient Greek mythology; the father of creation, the god of light, the god of sky, the god of the Sun, the god of the heavens and weather.

⭐ Zeus' favourite weapon was thunderbolts.

⭐ Zeus is an Olympian god who lived on the summit of Mount Olympus, Greece.

Coolness 10/10

If you're looking for nice gods, you'll be disappointed as only all-powerful gods of vengeance are here, those who walk a thin line between good and evil. They may be hard as nails and enjoy an unfair fight, but these deities are very cool! They also serve an important narrative function in world mythologies. After all, you can't have light without dark, and you can't be good if evil doesn't exist.

Mictlantecuhtli

★ God of the dead in Aztec mythology.

★ His name means 'Lord of Mictlan', the Aztec hell.

★ One of the principal gods of the Aztecs.

★ The worship of Mictlantecuhtli often involved ritual cannibalism.

Coolness 10/10

Anubis

★ In Ancient Egyptian mythology, Anubis is depicted with the head of a jackal or dog.

★ He also has the body of a human female.

★ He is associated with death and mummification.

★ The Egyptian Book of the Dead, an ancient funerary text, describes Anubis guiding the dead on their journey to the underworld.

Coolness 10/10

Apocalypse Now: Ragnarok

Death and destruction in the world's mythologies is everywhere, from epic battles to full-scale wars, and even the opening of Pandora's Box. Every mythology, on every continent, speaks of the coming Apocalypse. But when it comes to a mega-sized appetite for destruction, Norse mythology's account of the total annihilation of the world takes some beating ...

The Nine Worlds

According to Scandinavia's Norse mythology, Ragnarok will be the end of days for Earth, as well as the Nine Worlds, which are:

Asgard
The home of the Aesir.

Vanaheim
The home of the Vanir.

Alfheim
The home of the light elves.

Midgard
'Middle Earth', home of the humans, connected to Asgard by Bifrost – the Rainbow Bridge.

Jotunheim
Home of the giants.

Svartalfheim
Home of the dark elves.

Nidavellir
Home of the dwarves.

Niflheim
Home of the dead.

Muspelheim
Home of the fire giants and demons.

THE END IS NIGH

Ragnarok

The Nine Worlds (including Midgard, or Earth) will be destroyed during Ragnarok, meaning 'rain of the dust', a war that will bring untold death and destruction when the Norse gods wage the final battle with the giants. According to Norse mythology, the events leading up to Ragnarok have already been set in motion:

★ Before Ragnarok begins, Earth will suffer a winter of wars that will last three years.

★ Loki, Thor's brother and trickster, will gather the frost giants and sail to Asgard, the home of gods. Fenrir, Jormungand, and Hel will join Loki and other evil characters in a battle against Odin, Thor, Heimdell and the other gods.

★ On the morning of Ragnarok, Heimdall will sound his mighty horn, summoning the gods to battle.

★ During the battle all the great gods – including Odin, Loki and Thor – and the monsters, giants and evil beings of the Nine Worlds will be killed.

★ After the battle, Earth will be set on fire, the Sun and Moon will be destroyed, the sky will fall, and the world will sink beneath the sea and vanish forever.

★ However, Ragnarok will not be the end. The World Tree, Yggdrasill, will survive, as will two humans, Lif and Lifthrasir, who will repopulate the new world.

Hit or Myth

The ancient Greek myths may have given the English language the word 'apocalypse', but they didn't really tell stories about it. To them, the world had already ended, been destroyed, and been fought over many times in epic battles between the gods.

'I believe in everything until it's disproved.
So I believe in fairies, the myths, dragons.
It all exists, even if it's in your mind.
Who's to say that dreams and nightmares
aren't as real as the here and now?'

John Lennon

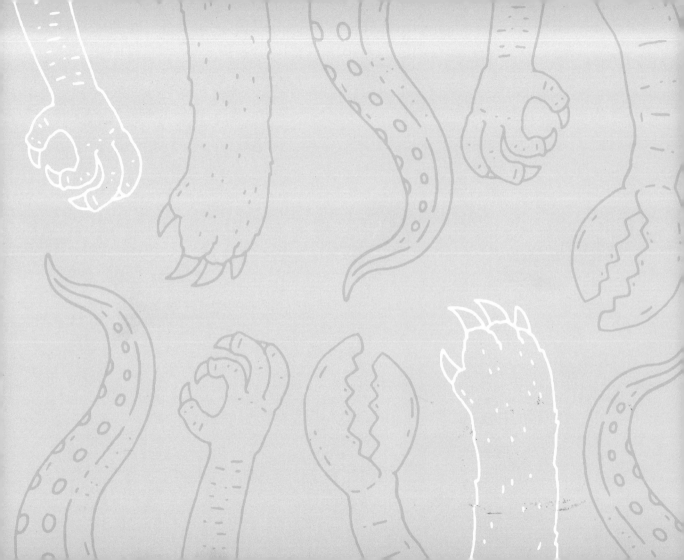